SHOWDOWN

Maule looked at Pete for long silent seconds, then he shook his head. "You beat up my man at night and then, by God, you've got the gall to hit me for a job next morning."

"Maybe I can take his place."

A look of anger washed over Maule's face and then he burst into laughter.

As if on signal, his three bodyguards laughed too, as if in anticipation of what was to come.

One man, the biggest of the three, unbuckled the wide belt of his trousers and began wrapping it around the palm of his right hand. The other two men rose.

Pete knew what was up. Two of them would hold him while the man with the belt-wrapped fist beat his face to a pulp. But he didn't know what Maule had in mind.

Maule watched him, his green eyes alert for Pete's reaction. "What do you say now, Brisbin?" He tilted his head toward the three waiting men.

Pete said calmly, "If they're going to do what I think they're going to do, the man with the strap is as good as dead."

THE
DESERTERS

LUKE SHORT

A DELL BOOK

Published by
Dell Publishing
a division of
Bantam Doubleday Dell Publishing Group, Inc.
666 Fifth Avenue
New York, New York 10103

ISBN: 0-440-20592-1

Reprinted by arrangement with the author's estate

Printed in the United States of America

Published simultaneously in Canada

May 1990

10 9 8 7 6 5 4 3 2 1

KRI

1

The thundering knock on the door of his room in the bachelor officers' quarters caught First Lieutenant Pete Brisbin as he was finishing shaving. The result was predictable and he nicked himself with his straight-edge.

"Come in," he called testily and reached for the towel on the washstand to blot up the drops of blood that began to trickle down over the shelf of his lean jaw. In the mirror past the reflection of an angry dark-haired young man, stripped to the waist and holding a towel to jaw, he saw the door open and observed Corporal Green come to attention, salute and then heard him say, "Major Horton's compliments, sir, and will you please report to him immediately?"

The Lieutenant grunted and then turned to regard the corporal. "Solly, ever try knocking on a door instead of trying to kick it down?"

"Thought you might be resting, sir, after morning drill."

"All right, all right. Tell the major I'll be over as soon as I tie off an artery." He looked at the offending corporal, then removed the towel from his jaw and looked at the bloodstain.

The corporal grinned. "Yes, sir." He saluted, stepped through the doorway and closed the door ever so gently behind him.

Lieutenant Brisbin rummaged around in the bag that held his shaving kit for the jar of powdered alum, wondering what Major Horton wanted and why he had to want it on a morning when his particular lieutenant had a thundering hangover and only three hours' sleep behind him.

As he applied the alum to the cut and felt its sting, he

reckoned that something had come through by telegraph from Department Headquarters or something had come in the morning's mail to warrant his immediate summons.

Disposing of his shaving water, he packed up his shaving kit, crossed the big room, skirted the cot of Lieutenant Evan Cross, his roommate, tossed the kit on his own cot and picked up his blouse and shrugged into it. The gold braid of his epaulets was tarnished which, tradition said, was the prerogative of an officer who had served in the field.

Lifting his battered cavalryman's hat off the nail over his bed, he moved out into the corridor, a tall young man, leaned to thinness, who had a scarcely perceptible limp.

The glare of the sun-baked parade ground slitted his gray eyes and tightened the throb of his headache. He tramped carefully in the shade of the adobe B.O.Q's *portal* and of the officers' mess behind it and then, running out of shade, he moved out into the blasting sun toward the adobe headquarters building adjoining the wide sentry gate.

The orderly room he entered held two desks, at one of which Corporal Green was seated. At the officer-of-the-day's desk closer to the rear wall, a blond young second lieutenant was seated. He and Lieutenant Brisbin stared at each other without greeting, for they had parted sometime around dawn.

"What's the beauty patch, Pete?" Lieutenant Markham asked.

Lieutenant Brisbin reached up to his jaw and gently rubbed away the alum. "Ask Solly," he said, then he asked, tilting his head toward the closed door in the left wall, "Anybody with him?"

"He's waiting for you," Corporal Green said.

Brisbin moved over to the door and, remembering Solly's assault on his own door, gave two conservative knocks and was bid enter. Taking off his hat, tucking it under his left arm, he went into the room, closed the door behind him, then walked toward the desk stretched across the far corner. Halting before it, he saluted Major Horton.

The major gave his salute a lazy acknowledgment and said, "Morning, Pete. Take a chair."

Major Horton was a heavy-set, balding man of forty-odd years, whose long face, sagging lower eyelids below soft brown eyes, full drooping mustaches and long ears gave him the aspect of an amiable bloodhound. Behind his desk was a standard holding the American flag and the guidon of the Third Cavalry. His desk was littered with papers and files. He watched Lieutenant Brisbin carefully as the young man said, "Good morning, sir," and then moved to the leather-padded armchair facing a corner of the desk and eased himself into it.

Wordlessly Major Horton leaned down, opened a drawer, lifted out a bottle of whisky and a glass and set it on the corner of the desk closest to the lieutenant.

"If you need it, help yourself, and I think you do."

Lieutenant Brisbin smiled faintly and said, "Is that an order, sir?"

"Definitely."

He watched as Lieutenant Brisbin reached out, took the bottle and glass, poured himself two fingers of bourbon, lifted the glass in acknowledgment, drank off the whisky and returned the bottle and glass to the desk. The major watched him with fond disapproval before saying, "That's the last one you'll have on this post for some time."

Brisbin was silent a moment trying to mask his surprise. "I'm being transferred, is that it, sir?"

"Not likely," the major said. "You're being detached for special duty at my request. Orders came through from Department Headquarters twenty minutes ago." When Brisbin only nodded, the major asked quietly, "Not even curious?"

"Of course I am, I—I was just surprised is all. For what special duty, sir?"

The major leaned back in his chair and said thoughtfully, "Let's see. This must have begun when you were in the Academy. Anyway, it was seven years ago, and if you've

ever heard of it, you've probably forgotten." He paused and
added, "I can assure you, I haven't."

Brisbin waited.

"I was stationed at Camp Stambaugh up in the South
Pass country in Wyoming territory. All around us there was
Indian trouble and we had our share of it. Along with that
trouble there came trouble from the toughs in the mining
camp close to us in South Pass City. Because of the Indian
trouble we hadn't been paid for months. No troopers could
be spared by the other posts to escort the paymaster. Finally, our C.O. took matters in his own hands. He sent a
detachment of his own men to Fort Laramie where the paymaster was hung up. A Lieutenant Gant headed the detail.
He was given Sergeant Fairly and eight experienced troopers. Remember that name—Fairly, Pete."

"First name, sir?"

"Jess. Jess Fairly. The detail made Laramie without any
trouble, picked up the paymaster and started back for Stambaugh. On the way back they ran into a carefully planned
ambush. It was in country too rough to put out flankers. At
least that's the assumption because all of Gant's detail were
lost—all except Fairly, that is."

"He escaped?" Brisbin asked.

"He planned it."

Brisbin frowned. "How can they be sure of that, sir?"

"There were a couple of immigrant wagons ahead of the
detail. They heard the shooting, figured it was Indians and
forted up. When nothing happened they went back down
the road. They found one trooper still alive. He said his
sergeant had shot him. He died while they were looking at
the others. The pay chest ironed to the daugherty wagon
was blown. According to information from Laramie there
was over twenty thousand in gold in the paymaster's chest."

"The paymaster was killed, of course?"

"Yes, he was an old friend of mine." He paused. "That's
the background."

The major leaned forward now and took a letter from a

pile of correspondence. "Two weeks ago I got this. It's from the corporal who was my company clerk. He served out his enlistment and I could not talk him into re-enlistment, but we were good friends and we correspond. This letter I'll give you to memorize. Briefly, he says he ran into Sergeant Fairly down at a mining camp in Arizona by the name of Banning. Fairly is a prosperous rancher, owns a good part of the town and has surrounded himself with hardcases."

"I see," Lieutenant Brisbin said slowly. "You want him back, is that it?"

Major Horton nodded. "Delivered in leg irons to the closest army post."

Lieutenant Brisbin hesitated a moment before saying, "May I make a suggestion, sir?" At Horton's nod, Brisbin continued, "Why doesn't this closest army post send out a detail and bring him in?"

Major Horton made a loose gesture toward the letter. "That will tell you. Sergeant Fairly is going by the name of Ben Maule down there. His ranch is close to the border, if any of the military show up in Banning or anywhere near it, Mr. Ben Maule drifts down into Mexico. He stays there till they're cleared out."

"Did Maule or Fairly recognize your company clerk?"

"He never got a chance to. The clerk figured, rightly enough, that if Fairly saw him he'd have him killed. After all, he and his toughs didn't stop at murdering the paymaster's escort, so what's one more dead man?"

Again Lieutenant Brisbin nodded. "What are your exact orders, sir?"

"Why, to go down there as a civilian, capture him and bring him to the nearest army post. In time, he'll be tried for complicity in murder. If that's unprovable he'll be tried for grand larceny and if that's unprovable he'll be tried as a deserter."

Lieutenant Brisbin thought this over for a few silent moments and then said, "May I ask another question, sir?"

"Anything you want."

"Do I have the requirements for this job?"

"You've already volunteered," the major said dryly.

"And why did I volunteer?" Lieutenant Brisbin asked with an equal dryness.

Major Horton looked at him levelly and then said in a matter-of-fact voice, "It is a matter of official record that your wife and infant daughter recently died in childbirth. You would like to be transferred from this post which was the scene of their death. I concurred by saying you were the top officer in grade under my command." He paused. "What I did not say was that if you keep on drinking and gambling and horseracing and general hell-raising, I will be forced to request that you be transferred out of my command for the good of its morale." He leaned forward and put his elbows on the desk and placed his hands palms down in the litter of paper work. "I volunteered you, and my request was accepted because Captain Hansom, the paymaster, was a friend and classmate of mine. I don't deny I am married to a woman whose father is a major general. Neither do I deny that he has a copy of all my messages regarding this matter to the Department of the Missouri. Any more questions, Pete?"

Lieutenant Brisbin rose. "No, sir. Thank you, sir," he said quietly.

The major picked up the envelope holding the company clerk's letter. He rose now, came around the desk, extended the letter, and then offered his hand to Lieutenant Brisbin who accepted it. "Good luck, Pete, and take care."

2

The mining camp of Banning was nestled at the mouth of a broad canyon at the foot of the skeleton bare Padres Mountains. From the map file at Fort Ely, Pete had learned that it was roughly seventy miles to the west from the *Rio Conejos,* on whose west bank was located Fort Lyman, the closest cavalry post. Banning was less than a decade old and was still partly a tent city, although most of its permanent buildings were one- and two-story adobes. Only the banks of the *acquias* that used to irrigate the small farms on the valley floor held a growth of shade and fruit trees. The timbered head frames of the mines scattered on the lower slopes of the spiny Padres had been freighted in, as had the posts which supported the *portals* of the business buildings that supplied blessed shade for pedestrians.

Pete Brisbin had expected to find a drowsy southwestern village which had adapted to the easygoing pace of the life below the border, a few miles away. Instead, he found himself amidst a tangle of freight and ore wagons on their way to and from the mines and the mills. This should be suppertime, for dusk was settling, but apparently this camp paid no attention to the clock. Everyone and everything moved in a perpetual cloud of dust that the teams of the wagons raised on the wide main street.

Finding a feed stable was his first order of business, and in the fourth block of the business section of the town he found one. The stable itself was of adobe and so was the big corral. Pete turned his bay gelding purchased two days back over to a Mexican hostler with orders to grain him, and then sought the street. He was dressed in worn levis and a sun-faded calico shirt; with his scuffed cowman's boots and a week's dark beard stubble, to anyone observing him and the worn shell belt and holstered gun, he was just another drifting cowhand.

In the short time it had taken to find a feed stable and leave his horse, dusk had settled and the lamps were already burning in some of the stores. Remembering the company clerk's letter, which he had memorized and returned to Major Horton, he knew that his curiosity alone would take him first to Ben Maule's big Crossfire Saloon. It was, the clerk had written, aptly named, for trouble seemed to gravitate there.

As he made his way on the packed earth sidewalk under a succession of *portals,* he noted that while many people in the crowd were Mexican, the majority seemed to be miners of foreign extraction. They wore heavy boots and trousers, usually held up by suspenders, and round black wool hats. Some carried dinner buckets, but whether they were going on shift or coming off, he couldn't tell.

Then he caught sight of the Crossfire down the street, a big, high, one-story adobe. Kerosene flares on either side of the big open doorway lighted the entrance. As he picked his course between the wagons and crossed the street, he could hear the din made by the hundred voices inside the saloon. Heading for the saloon's doors, he noticed that wire mesh covered the big windows both inside and out. And then the pandemonium he stepped into was almost like a physical blow. The room was huge and a bar ran the length of the room on the left. No bottles were in sight and there was no back bar mirror to be shattered in the endless fights. A half-dozen shirt-sleeved bartenders were serving the men who jammed the bar for its entire length. On the right side of the room there were four big round card tables and all their chairs were occupied. There were two faro layouts against the rear wall, and perched on a high stool behind it was a watcher with a shotgun across his lap. The high ceiling from which a dozen overhead pull-down lamps hung was almost invisible through the curtain of tobacco smoke.

Pete moved to the bar and finally caught a bartender's attention and asked for a beer. After paying for it, he moved, beer mug in hand, through the crowd. On his way toward the rear, a cruising houseman in a white shirt with a sawed-off pool cue in hand passed him. A fight erupted in the doorway behind him and two burly housemen bowled their way through the crowd toward it. Some of the drinkers, Pete noted, were very drunk, but the bartenders served them as long as they could hold a glass.

Pete slowly pushed his way back toward the faro layout, which was getting a big play, and was surprised to see that the faro dealer was a handsome red-haired woman in her early thirties. He had heard of professional women gamblers, but this was the first one he had ever seen, and a more incongruous and inelegant setting for her he couldn't imagine.

He moved closer now to get a look at her. She had, like most professional gamblers, an utterly expressionless face and never bothered to look at the players who were betting. Win or lose, she showed no emotion as the case tender called the cards as they came out of the case in a husky, indifferent voice. The sleeves of her green blouse were elbow length and around its neck was a sunburst of white lace.

Pete asked the man beside him, "Who's she?"

"I dunno. Everybody calls her Lace."

Obviously she was everybody's favorite, since the cursing and swearing was held to a minimum by the losing players.

Pete was watching the play when he heard a twangy voice that carried over the din of the room. "You, cowboy. Bet or move off."

Pete shuttled his glance to the watcher with the shotgun who was looking directly at him. He was an old man with bleach eyes and a drooping mustache that didn't succeed in hiding a thin-lipped, mean mouth.

Pete raised his half-full mug of beer to acknowledge he had heard and then remained where he was. He was not disturbing the play and he was a patron of the house. He shuttled his glance back to the woman and continued to watch. He was aware now of a piercing whistle that carried over the clamor of the room, but it seemed only another noise added to the many.

It could have been five or ten seconds after he had heard and forgotten the whistle that he felt a hand roughly grab his arm. He turned and saw a burly white-shirted houseman, a sawed pool cue trailing from his other hand.

"All right, you. Outside," the houseman said roughly.

"Front or back?" he asked innocently.

"It don't matter. Get out."

"Or you'll do what?"

The men closest to them started to push away, sensing trouble. The very fact they did so exposed Pete's back to the watcher with the shotgun. Somehow Pete knew he had to maneuver the houseman between him and the watcher. But above all he had to call attention to himself, had to get things in motion if he was ever to meet Ben Maule. This was the opportunity.

"Want me to show you?" the houseman asked as he began to raise the pool cue.

Pete, his half-filled beer mug held at his chest, shrugged and started past the houseman toward the front door. As Pete moved even with him, he swiftly tossed the beer into the houseman's face and eyes. That second of the burly man's blindness gave Pete the time he needed. He moved to the side of the houseman, who was now between him and the watcher.

Recovering quickly, the houseman gave a backhanded side swipe with the pool cue, aiming at Pete's head. Pete moved the beer mug slightly away from him, rigidly steadied it and let the back of the houseman's hand slam into it. The drive of the blow shattered the heavy glass.

Reflexively, reacting to the pain, the houseman's hand opened and the pool cue sailed harmlessly into the midriff of a watching miner. Still blinking beer from his eyes, surprised and hurt, the houseman lifted his arm to look at the gash across his hand. At the same time came the watcher's shrill whistle. Before the houseman could look away from his hand, Pete lifted his leg and sent his boot heel crashing down on the instep of the houseman's right foot. This brought a bray of anguish from the houseman, who lifted his leg to ease the pain.

With the houseman standing barely balanced on one leg, Pete drove his fist into the hinge of the houseman's jaw just below his ear. Pete felt something give under his fist and then saw the houseman, driven off balance, begin to topple over.

Swiftly, Pete dived into the crowd and roughly shouldered his way toward the door in the back of the big room. He looked at the watcher and saw that the older man was standing, shotgun half raised to his shoulder. Because Pete was taller than the average man, he could see the watcher and the watcher could see him, but Pete knew that unless the watcher was truly insane, he would not dare to shoot into this mob and kill or wound three or four men.

Approaching the door in the rear, Pete saw a few feet of open space which would give the watcher the chance he wanted.

Without even thinking, Pete seized the nearest miner by the back of his belt and his shirt collar, hoisting him off his feet, and then, using him as a shield between himself and the watcher, he stumbled to the open doorway. Safe here, he dropped the struggling miner and then headed down a dimly lit corridor off which were rooms on either side, their doors closed. Pete ran for the black rectangle of the open back door and, as he made it, could hear the pounding of booted feet behind him. He dodged left on the heel of a gunshot from inside and abruptly ran into a stack of empty beer barrels, caromed off them into a dark alley, heard a couple of them fall, and then he was running down the alley.

While it was not totally dark, he had a feeling of complete helplessness, for he was a total stranger to the buildings and layout of the town.

Looking over his shoulder now, he saw men pouring out of the saloon back doorway. He turned and ran faster, and then, where the alley opened out onto the dimly lighted side street, he saw two men break off their running to halt at the alley mouth ahead of him. They listened. Pete, knowing they were trying to pick up the sound of his running, halted too. One man started down the alley, the other resumed his running up the side street.

Pete looked across the alley and saw a dark rectangle between two buildings. A passageway? he wondered. He cut across the alley, and with hands outstretched, walked into the black rectangle. It appeared to be a walkway between two adobe buildings. At its far end there was diffused light which probably came from a street ahead paralleling the alley.

Carefully he moved down the weed-cluttered passageway. He heard the sound of men running in the alley now, and flattened himself against the wall, afraid they might pick up his silhouette against the light from the other street. When they had passed, he heard their muffled shouts, and he moved carefully toward the distant street. He passed what in the darkness he took to be a window in the wall on his left. He was only a few feet beyond it when, at the far end of the passageway, he saw a figure stop, then start down the walkway toward him.

He was concerned. He had his choice of overpowering by gun or fist the man coming toward him, or he could take a chance on retreating to the alley. When he looked back at the alley, he saw the dim light growing ever stronger and he knew his pursuers had rounded up lanterns.

Then he remembered the window in the wall. Moving back toward it, he halted by it and gingerly extended his hand. It was a window and it was open, drawn curtains behind it. Looking toward the street now, he saw his man distantly silhouetted against the light and he knew he had no choice. Carefully, then, he parted the curtains and silently climbed into the window and let the curtains fall closed behind him.

The darkness here was absolute and he didn't move. Listening, he could hear the muted shouts of men in the alley. Stilling his breath, he waited for the sound of the man coming along the walkway. The sounds did not come. Was the man waiting for the others with lanterns to flush him out?

And then a voice from inside the room came to him. "Whoever you are, go out the way you came. I have a gun and I can see you."

It was the voice of a frightened woman.

Pete waited a long moment before answering. "I won't hurt you, but I can't go out. They're hunting me."

"Stay where you are." The faint creaking of leather webbing bed straps came from across the room, then a rustle of cloth, then a rasping of a match and the room was lighted. Pete saw a slight figure, back to him, touch the match to the lamp and replace the chimney, then turn up the wick. Afterward, she picked up a pistol from the night table and stepped to one side of the lamp to put its light on him. They regarded each other in silence, both surprised.

By the light of the lamp, Pete saw a slight girl, twin braids of blond hair falling over each shoulder. The sight of it was oddly heart-wrenching, for this was the way his wife, Anne, had fixed her hair for sleep, a poignant holdover from childhood. This girl wore a blue wrapper and he noted irrelevantly that the toes of her bare feet were curled up away from the chill of the earth floor. Her face was thin enough to make her dark eyes seem wide and unblinking, but perhaps it was only her surprise and fright.

"Who's hunting you?"

"Why, the housemen at the Crossfire, I reckon. I didn't stay to see."

There were muffled shouts from the alley and now Pete turned his head and saw there was a door leading from this room into the alley. The girl looked at the door too, and then she waved her gun, saying, "Get over in that corner and away from the window."

Pete moved past a plain wooden dresser to the corner, which was curtained off and which he judged was her closet.

Now she put the gun on the table, picked up the lamp and moved over to the alley door. After unlocking it, she opened it, screening Pete from the alley. Then she stepped forward, blocking Pete's view of her. The sound of men talking outside died.

"What's all the row out here?" she called, almost angrily.

There was a pause and then a voice said, "We're looking for a man, Miss Laurie."

"Do you have to wake the dead doing it?"

Another male voice asked, "You seen anything of him, Miss Laurie? A tall cowboy, he was."

"How could I?" Laurie answered tartly. "I was sleeping till your racket woke me up. Now clear out of here and do your carousing somewhere else."

She didn't wait for their answer but slammed the door and locked it, then stayed there listening. There was a low murmur of talk outside which presently trickled off into silence.

She turned her head now and looked at Pete, who said, "They seem to know you. Laurie what?" Then he added, "I'm Pete Brisbin."

"Laurie Mays. Yes, they know me. I run a boarding and rooming house with my aunt."

She turned now and went back to the night stand and set the lamp on it. Pete moved over to the middle of the room and when she turned to look at him again, he said, "You didn't have to do that, but I'm much obliged." He hesitated. "Why did you?"

"Why, if those bully boys at the Crossfire are after you, you must have hit one of them to make them mad. They're a pack of brutes to a man, so you must be all right."

Pete nodded and grinned. "Where is your rooming house, Miss Laurie?"

"Why, you're in it. Come to think of it, you're in my bedroom where you don't belong."

"Are you filled up?"

"Except one room. Why?"

"Well, you're filled up now. If you'll show me my room, I'll get out of yours."

Laurie Mays laughed and it was a delight to hear her, Pete thought. All the sternness and suspicion and the tension fled from her face. It was the face now of a gentle, humorous and overworked girl in her twenties.

Laurie sat down on the bed now, leaned over and pulled on a pair of low-cut Indian moccasins, then stood up and picked up the lamp.

"Aunt Martha won't believe this, and I won't tell her. I'll say that she must have slept through the night bell, that I heard it and found you in the hall."

"Well, it does sound more logical," Pete conceded and they smiled at each other.

Laurie, lamp in hand, opened the door on the other side of the night table and stepped into a roomy kitchen. Crossing it, she led the way past a dining room holding two big tables, then into a lamplit corridor. Under the stairs was a key rack, from which Laurie took a key and handed it to Pete. "It's upstairs. Number seven by the bracket lamp. Room and board for a week is ten dollars, for a month thirty-five."

Pete reached in his pocket, drew out an eagle and handed it to Laurie.

"Let's say a week." At her nod, he asked, "Could I talk to you in the morning?"

Laurie nodded. "While I'm making up the rooms," she said matter-of-factly. "Breakfast is at six. If you hear a racket during the night, that will be Mr. Moynihan falling down stairs. He gets taken down drunk about every third night, so pay no attention. Good night, Mr. Brisbin."

3

Breakfast was at the early hour promised, for most of Laurie Mays's boarders were connected in minor supervisory capacities with the mines and mills, whose day shifts began at seven o'clock. Laurie's Aunt Martha turned out to be a rawboned, gray-haired, no-nonsense woman who, along with a sturdy Mexican woman, ran the kitchen.

It was a good and plentiful breakfast and Pete took his time about eating it, so that when Laurie, who was the waitress besides being the housekeeper, poured his second cup of coffee, all the others had gone and the table was cleared. Laurie brought her own cup of coffee, pulled out a chair and sat down, saying, "I got to thinking about it. You can't trail me around the rooms asking questions, so ask them now. What do you want to know?"

"Do the men that own the mines mostly live here in town, Miss Laurie?"

"Some do, but the rich owners have turned theirs over to the superintendents and left. Are you a miner?" When Pete shook his head in negation, she added, "But you're looking for work?"

"That's what I was getting around to. Who's hiring men to do what?"

"Well, Mr. Moynihan says there's a big turnover in teamsters that freight out the ore. Not many of them can work very long in the dust of the roads. It gets to their lungs and their eyes get running sores and finally they have to quit."

"Are there ranches around?"

Laurie nodded. "They hire mostly Mexican hands, though." Now Laurie frowned thoughtfully. "There's one man you could see, only last night spoiled that."

Pete frowned. "How?"

"Well, he owns the Crossfire, two mines, a custom mill and a general store. If you hit a man last night in the saloon, it was one of his. If you hurt him badly you might be in for trouble."

"Who's this you're talking about?"

"Ben Maule, he's called."

"And where do I find him?"

Laurie smiled faintly. "That's just it. His office is in a back room of the Crossfire. You wouldn't make it much past the front door."

Pete was silent a moment and then asked, "Do you know him?"

Laurie took a sip of her coffee, put her cup down and said, "Oh, yes. Outside of the miners that just come and go, everyone knows everyone else in this town."

"Could I say you sent me?"

Laurie's dark eyes widened in surprise and she said, "What good would that do you?"

"When I see him I've got to say something. If I say you sent me to him there's a connection started. Otherwise, I'm just a drifter off the streets."

"I can see that," Laurie said slowly.

"Maybe you'd rather not get involved," Pete said.

"I don't call that being involved," Laurie said. "I simply told you to see him because he has a lot of irons in the fire. Yes, you can use my name for what it's worth. After all, we do trade at his store." She stood up and said, "I must get to work. Good luck."

Pete rose too, carried his cup into the kitchen and set it down on the sink drainboard beside the Mexican woman who was washing the dishes. They exchanged smiles and then Pete nodded, said, "Good day," to Aunt Martha and sought the street.

He paused under the *portal* and ran a hand over his beard-stubbled cheek. Should he get his blanket roll at the feed stable, return, shave and put on a clean shirt before his interview, or appear just as he was? If Ben Maule was a former army sergeant, although a crooked killer of a one, he would have expected a clean and orderly appearance in his men while on garrison duty. Still, he wouldn't expect that same appearance from a drifter cowpuncher. No, he would go as he was.

He moved down to the corner under the *portal* and took the side street that lay a block off the main street. Everything that Laurie had told him about Maule only confirmed the contents of the company clerk's letter. Now he was about to test further the accuracy of the letter. 'Surrounded by hardcases,' the letter had said.

From a half-block distance, Pete could see the curtain of dust that already hung over the main street. When he reached it, he saw that the miners, their faces grimy, and carrying dinner pails, were coming off from night shift. The majority of them wearily headed for their tent dormitories or sleazy rooms. Some, Pete noticed, were turning into the Crossfire for some drinking before they crawled into their lice-ridden blankets.

There was nowhere near the crowd in the Crossfire that there had been last evening, but it was doing a good business at this early hour. Was it too early for Maule? he wondered.

Of the nearest bartender he asked, "Mr. Maule come in yet?"

"You're half an hour early," the bartender said.

Pete nodded and sought the street. He was just as glad that he was early because it would give him a chance to get a look at Ben Maule before talking with him. Of course, Maule could use the back entrance to the Crossfire, but Pete reasoned that as an owner of a saloon, he would probably use the front entrance and check on the business, bartenders and the previous night's damage, if any.

The wagon traffic was slowly building up to its usual steady flow and Pete watched it, not knowing exactly what he was looking for, but certain that he would know it when he saw it. A drink of whisky, if only to wash his teeth, would be a welcome thing, but then he remembered his last visit with Major Horton. It was true that during these months since Anne's death he had been overdrinking. Whisky was no particular solace, but it did seem to dull the edge of the quiet grief that was always with him. The whisky and the late card games and the company of the other junior officers were only time users and time deadeners, and while they hadn't affected his performance as an officer, they hadn't helped either.

And then this reverie was broken by what he saw on the street. Between two ore wagons came a group of five riders, all dressed in range clothes and all wearing neckerchiefs pulled up to below their eyes. They were all armed, pistols at hip, carbines in their saddle scabbards. The placing of their mounts—two abreast ahead of one alone and two bringing up the rear—suggested the rider in the middle was being guarded or protected. This was a big man, a heavy man, and when they pulled in to the tie rail in front of the Crossfire and paralleling it, the two leaders and the big man and one of the drag riders dismounted. The fifth rider accepted the reins of the other four riders, then the big man with his three guards went through the break in the tie rail and entered the Crossfire, while the fourth rider leading the four mounts rode down the street, probably to the feed stable.

Pete pushed away from the wall, ducked under the tie rail and waited for a huge ore wagon with its three teams of mules to pass him. His look at Ben Maule had not revealed much except that he was a bear of a man, and afraid for his life.

When the high-wheeled ore wagon passed, Pete cut across the road and entered the Crossfire, pulling down his neckerchief as he moved down the bar. Ahead of him behind the dozen men along the bar, he saw the last of Maule's bodyguard disappear in the dark back corridor.

There was one lone puncher at the end of the bar apparently waiting to attract the bartender's attention. Without knowing for sure, Pete guessed this was one of the body-guards, dropped out to watch the corridor.

Pete angled toward him and halted under his cold stare. He was a leathery bleach-eyed man, shorter than Pete and ten years his senior, who wore a gun on his left hip.

"I'd like to see Mr. Maule," Pete said civilly.

"He ain't here," the puncher said flatly.

Pete regarded him carefully, then tilted his head toward the corridor doorway. "I saw him go in there."

"No you never."

Patiently Pete said, "Look, Lefty, I'll give you one more chance. Go back and tell him there's a man out here that Miss Laurie Mays sent."

"What if I don't?"

"I reckon you will," Pete said quietly. "I don't like trouble, but I don't mind it. You likely feel the same way."

"I don't mind it even a little bit." The puncher pushed away from the bar and for a fleeting second Pete wondered if trouble wasn't right here.

"Now don't get spooky," the puncher added. "I'm going to lift your gun."

"Go ahead."

The puncher casually lifted Pete's gun from his holster, then turned and walked back into the dark corridor. Pete knew that the mention of Laurie Mays's name had turned the trick. Whether it would turn it with Ben Maule was another thing.

A bartender came up to Pete's place at the bar and said, "What'll it be, mister?"

Pete turned to him and said, "Nothing. I'm waiting."

The bartender nodded and looked at him searchingly, then, instead of going back up the bar, he slowly moved down it and sauntered into the corridor. It was so dark in the corridor that Pete could see nothing and he wondered why there was no lamp in it or why someone did not open the back door to light it.

There was a long wait and then the bartender, wiping his

hands on his soiled apron, reappeared, and went behind the bar and past Pete without giving him a glance.

Moments later the puncher appeared in the doorway, raised a hand and beckoned Pete toward him. As Pete approached, the puncher turned and led the way down the dark corridor. At the rearmost room on the left he opened the door without knocking and, saying nothing to Pete, he moved into the room. Pete trailed him.

Across the room was a large rectangular black-topped desk, situated so that the man who sat behind it had a clear view of the corridor door and the two windows that faced the alley. The lower halves of these two windows were whitewashed to make them opaque.

His guide and the other two bodyguards were seated in barrel chairs against the wall to the left and Pete put his attention on the big man seated behind the paper-littered desk. He noted that his own pistol lay on the desk top.

Ben Maule, besides having a big body, had a big head covered with kinky red hair to go with it. His broad Irish face held the scars of many a long-gone barroom scrap and his short wide-nostrilled nose, probably flattened in a fight, had been reset imperfectly, so that it was faintly crooked. His wide mouth was thin-lipped and pleasant, verging on a smile. His green eyes, however, under great tufts of red eyebrows, were as cold and appraising as any horse trader's. He was, Pete judged, a strong and capable man gone wrong.

"Morning, Mr. Maule," Pete said.

Maule nodded. "You said Laurie Mays sent you to me. Why?"

"To ask you for work. She said you owned or had shares in a lot of businesses here in Banning and outside."

"You don't look like a miner or a prospector. You don't talk like one either."

Pete had long ago decided there was no sense in trying to hide the fact that he had some education, because eventually he would give himself away. Now he said forthrightly, "I was a schoolteacher."

One of the three men against the wall laughed shortly and contemptuously. Maule's look silenced him abruptly, and then he returned his attention to Pete. "Why aren't you now?"

"Trouble."

This brought the faintest of smiles from Maule. "I thought all schoolteachers were women."

"Not in a men's prison."

Surprise and possibly respect was reflected in Maule's face. He said then, "I didn't know there were teachers in any prison."

"There was at this one. You can't give orders to a foreigner who doesn't understand your language, so you teach it to him. That's what our warden thought anyway."

Maule leaned back in his chair and asked quietly, "Did you teach the prisoners how to beat up a man like you beat up my houseman last night?"

The bartender had recognized him, Pete thought. He said unsmilingly, "No, the prisoners taught me how to."

Maule's voice was suddenly cold as he asked, "What was that all about?"

"I bought a beer and was watching the faro. Your watcher told me to bet or move on. I wasn't crowding the players so I stayed. The watcher whistled in the houseman and he told me to get out. I hadn't even finished my beer. You know the rest."

Maule nodded. "I know you broke his jaw and his foot."

"That's a hard way to learn some manners," Pete said.

Maule looked at him for long silent seconds, then he shook his head as if in wonder. "You beat up my houseman at night and then, by God, you've got the gall to hit me for a job next morning."

"Maybe I can take his place."

A look of anger washed over Maule's face and then he burst into laughter.

As if on signal, the other three men laughed. Pete guessed that Maule's laughter was genuine, but the laughter of the other three was derisive, as if in anticipation of what was to come.

One man, the biggest of the three, rose out of his chair, took off his shell belt, and then unbuckled the wide belt of his trousers. Holding out the belt, he began wrapping it around the palm of his right hand. The other two men rose.

Pete knew what they had in mind. Two of them would haul him out into the alley and hold him while the man with the belt-wrapped fist beat his face to a pulp. But he didn't know what Maule had in mind.

He looked at Maule now and Maule watched him, his green eyes alert for Pete's reaction. Maule said then, "I don't even know your name." When Pete told him, Maule said, "What do you say now, Brisbin?" He tilted his head toward the three waiting men.

Pete said calmly, "If they're going to do what I think they're going to do, the man with the strap is as good as dead."

The three men waited, looking at Maule, who was still watching Pete. Maule said slowly, "I think you mean it."

"He'd better believe I do."

Maule turned his head and said, "Put it back, Beach. We've got a new houseman." To Pete he said, "See Josh Eddy before four. He runs this place."

Pete nodded and said, "Much obliged," turned and went out. Once on the street, he pulled up his neckerchief against the dust and headed for the feed stable. The first part of his job, the next to the hardest, was accomplished. He would be close to Ben Maule now and have access to him in the days ahead. How he could pry him away from his ever-present bodyguards, he could not tell. Yet.

As he tramped down the street, he thought back over the conversation in Maule's office. Just what, he wondered, had saved him from the beating he had earned? He suspected it was his lie that he had been in prison. Maule, of course, hated all authority or he would never have pulled off his paymaster's robbery. A crook tends to sympathize with a crook, even if an unsuccessful one. And the fact that Pete had done time was proof that he was not afraid to break the law.

At the feed stable he made arrangements for boarding his horse, and afterward he took his blanket roll and walked back to his rooming house.

Once in his room, he stripped off his shirt, took his shaving kit from his blanket roll and was lathering his face at the washstand before the mirror when he heard steps in the hall. They halted at his open door and before he could turn, Laurie said, "You're shaving in cold water. Let me get you some hot from downstairs."

"It's not all that cold, Miss Laurie."

Laurie glanced at the unrolled blanket roll on the bed which held nothing but a change of shirts and socks.

"I could iron you a shirt before you talk with Ben Maule if you'd like."

"I've seen him and I've got myself a job, so don't bother."

"Oh!" Laurie exclaimed, not pretending to hide her surprise. "Doing what?"

"Well, I kind of hurt one of his housemen yesterday. I offered to replace him."

Shaving brush in hand, lather drying on his face, Pete told of his interview with Maule witnessed by his hardcase bodyguards. As he talked, Laurie came into the room and sat on the edge of the bed, listening attentively. He finished by saying that it was her name that gave him access to Maule and his lying appeared to do the rest. When he had ceased talking, Laurie, hands folded in the lap of her gray working dress, said, "Well, I suppose you need the money."

"Because I'll take that sort of job, you mean?"

Laurie nodded. "You know what I think of those housemen. That's why I hid you from them last night."

"But I don't have to be like them."

Laurie nodded soberly. "But they all seem alike, Pete. You know they have to travel the streets in pairs and carry guns. If the miners caught one alone, they'd kill him. They're the most hated men in this camp."

"But I can handle a drunk without hurting him."

"If Josh Eddy will let you," Laurie said tartly.

Pete moved over to the washbowl and rinsed the lather from his face. His shave could wait. As he was toweling his face, he said, "What about this Eddy? I'm supposed to report to him at four o'clock."

"Well, when we first came to this camp he was a dealer in one of the gambling houses. Ben Maule took care of that. He closed it down like he had all the others. Have you noticed the Crossfire is the only saloon in town, except the hotel saloon?"

"I wondered about that. How did Maule do it?"

"His toughs would stage a fake fight that would simply wreck the place. They'd break windows, mirrors, chairs, tables and the bar. When the place was rebuilt, they'd do it again. The saloon people asked the sheriff to post Maule's men. He wouldn't do it because he's Maule's man himself. Ben Maule wanted the monopoly on the gambling and drinking and he got it, except for the hotel." She shrugged. "Maule didn't want the white-collar trade. He wanted the miners because they'd drink his rotten whisky and play his crooked games and if they objected he had the men to beat them up. He hired Josh Eddy to run the Crossfire."

She rose now and said, almost with resignation, "Well, you're one of his toughs now, Pete. I hoped it would be something else."

"He can't make me do anything I don't want to do. At least nobody has so far."

Laurie smiled faintly. "We'll see."

When Laurie had gone, Pete lathered his face again and as he shaved, pondered what she had told him. It seemed as if Ben Maule ran this town pretty much as he liked and he wondered why Maule was tolerated. Other mining camps faced with a similar situation had formed vigilante committees and cleaned out the roughs. Perhaps Maule hadn't pushed things too far. It was even possible that it would be more trouble to get rid of him than to tolerate him, especially if the sheriff was Maule's man and wouldn't cooperate in running him out.

Finished shaving, Pete went out on the town. He spent the rest of the morning walking the streets of the business district. From a block on either side of the dusty main street, the town and surroundings were only a collection of squalid tents and tent dormitories, cheap adobe rooming houses and occasional tar-paper shacks. The two-story adobe hotel on a side street was called The Bonanza, a pleasant-looking place with shrubs and flowers in its courtyard that Pete could see through a wide double-doored gate. Across from it, wedged between a harness and saddle shop and a bakery, was a single-story adobe building bearing over its doorway a sign proclaiming it the sheriff's office. Properly, Pete knew, it should have read DEPUTY SHERIFF'S OFFICE, for the county seat of Indian Bend was a good seventy miles to the west.

After a noon meal in a Mexican *cantina* that left his mouth burning and eyes watering, he rode out to the barren Padres and had a look at the outbuildings of a dozen mines on its slopes before turning back to town, putting up his horse and heading for the Crossfire and Josh Eddy.

The Crossfire held only a few patrons, for at this hour most of its customers were mucking out ore or freighting it to the mills. Of the nearest bartender, Pete asked where he could find Josh Eddy and was told that his office was across the corridor from Maule's.

Against the heat of the afternoon, the rear door he had escaped through last night was open, so there was light in the corridor. At his knock on the half-open door, a man's voice told him to come in.

Pete pushed the door fully open and stepped into the room. Directly ahead of him sat the faro dealer called Lace, and Pete removed his hat. At a flat counting table stacked with coins, his back to the window, sat Josh Eddy and Pete said, "Mr. Eddy, Mr. Maule told me to check in with you before four."

With nothing more to go on than Laurie's few words regarding Eddy, Pete was genuinely astonished at the sight of the man. He was pale, half bald, dumpy, and wore gold-rimmed glasses, the sort of man he might expect to find in the cashier's cage of a bank except that he was in shirt sleeves. Eddy now leaned back in his chair and said with some amusement, "That's the first time I've been called mister since I got fined in court. My name is Josh, hers is Lace Ferrill."

Pete nodded to the woman, who was coolly appraising him behind her expression of amusement. "And who are you?" she asked.

Eddy answered for her. "He's Pete Brisbin and he's taking Micky Howard's place. Matter of fact, he's the one that put Micky in Dock Price's back room." He looked at Pete, his shrewd brown eyes measuring the six feet of heavy bone and hard muscle under the careless range clothes. "Sit down," he said, nodding toward a straight-backed chair on Pete's left. Then he added, "You think you got enough heft?"

"Well, Micky wasn't light exactly," Pete said, and moved over to the chair and sat down.

Eddy said, "First thing you do when you leave here is to buy some white shirts. That's what you'll wear while you're working here."

"Why's that?" Pete asked.

"So you can spot the housemen if they need help and they can spot you if you do. Our customers sure as hell don't wear 'em."

Eddy laughed at his own joke and Lace Ferrill joined him with a throaty chuckle. Pete noticed that her high-necked amber-colored blouse was fringed with a paler colored lace.

"Just what's my job?" Pete asked.

"Why, you break up fights and throw out drunks. You

might say you help keep the peace, if you can call that bear pit peaceful out there."

"Do I pack a gun?"

"No. In that mob it's too easy to lift it off you. You pack a sawed-off pool cue and a knife in your pants pocket. Don't forget you're dealing with a bunch of hardheaded Hunkies, Wops and Micks. They got skulls two inches thick and they wear those thick wool hats mostly, so it takes a real belt to knock 'em down."

Pete nodded but made no comment and Eddy continued, "What comes first, though, is keeping an eye on Lace. Most of these miners have never seen a woman that don't have a handkerchief over her head and was wearing men's boots. They gamble just to get a close-up look at her. That brings the money in, but a lot of them want to take her home with them. That's why Hagerty—he's the lookout—whistled Micky Howard on you last night. When that move is on, she'll give the signal. Show him, Lace."

Pete looked at Lace. She raised her right hand to the lace at her throat.

Josh Eddy continued, "When you see that signal, come arunning." He paused. "What else do you want to know?"

"Are the games honest?" Pete asked bluntly.

Eddy said, "I'll pretend you didn't ask that."

"You've got no dealers for the table games, I noticed."

"One for poker, the others are too much trouble," Eddy said, and he shrugged. "A table is ten dollars an hour and ten percent of everyone's winnings. One of the housemen, Bill Shields, takes care of that. A dealer would have to know not only poker, but the card games of a dozen foreign countries. What the miners do, they buy a table to play their own home games. It beats gambling in a tent on a blanket by candlelight and here the booze is always handy." He paused. "What else?"

"This lookout, Hagerty," Pete said. "What number shot is in his gun?"

"Bird shot in a twenty gauge."

"In that jam he could blind a man or two or three," Pete said.

"That happens sometimes," Eddy conceded and let it rest there.

"What's so bad about that?" Lace said in her husky voice. "Every day on every shift those miners risk a hung shot, or a cave-in, or a rock fall or no air. Half of them are already crippled. Every time they go in a mine they don't know what to expect. Here they know if they get out of line there's a shotgun. That's more fair, isn't it?"

"But they're not drunk in a mine," Pete said.

"Some are, but that's their lookout," Lace countered.

She rose and smoothed out her black skirt over her thighs. "I've got to buy some food, Josh. I'll see you later." Her glance shuttled to Pete, who rose from his chair. "I'll be seeing you later, Pete," she said.

She went out, leaving the door open behind her, and Pete remained standing.

"What else?" Eddy asked.

"Nothing."

"Oh, but there is," Eddy said. He leaned forward and put his arms on the table. "In case you like the looks of that girl that just left the room, forget it. In case you'd like to walk her home, forget that too, and in case you'd like to talk with her about anything besides business, don't."

Pete was silent a moment, watching him. "Why?"

"She's Ben Maule's girl."

Pete nodded. "Since I can't ask her, maybe I can ask you. If you were a good-looking girl that liked to gamble, would you pick the Crossfire to work in?"

"Yes, if Ben Maule owned it," Eddy said coldly. When Pete said nothing, Eddy said, "Go get your white shirts." He stood up. "You don't ask me, so I won't tell you what your pay is. You'll work from four till midnight, except Saturday. You might work the whole night then."

"Why midnight on the other days?"

"Gentlemen's agreement," Eddy said. "The mines have

got to be worked and a drunk miner is useless. With five to six hours of sleep he'll show up sober."

"Maule owns a mine, I've heard."

Eddy nodded and said, "That's why it's midnight."

Pete nodded. "I'll see you later, then."

Eddy smiled faintly. "Not much later. I leave at six. After that, you five boys in the white shirts and the bartenders run the Crossfire."

Pete nodded and went out.

4

Pete bought a knife and his white shirts and changed into one in the alley, left the others and his gun and shell belt in Eddy's empty office and then moved out into the big barroom. The heat of the day was beginning to slack off and the customers, who were townsmen, began to drift in ahead of the miners who would soon be off shift and jamming the place.

From the same officious bartender who had tattled on him this morning, he asked where he could find the sawed-off pool cue he'd been told to carry.

"You want one with a wrist thong or without?"

"Which do you like?" Pete asked.

"Without," the bartender answered. "You get a wrist thong and they grab your club, they can tear your arm off."

"Then one without."

The bartender reached under the bar, made his selection and laid the sawed-off pool cue on the bar top. Pete asked for a beer, and while the bartender was drawing it, Pete surveyed the room. A dealer and case tender was setting up the faro layout that wasn't Lace's, under the idle surveillance of another houseman in a white shirt. Two other housemen were cruising the bar, stopping occasionally to exchange words with acquaintances.

The bartender returned with Pete's beer and when he offered to pay for it, the bartender said, "Forget it." As he spoke, one of the housemen passed behind Pete. He didn't speak and the bartender made no effort to halt him and introduce him to Pete.

Pete had taken only a couple of pulls at his beer when the second white-shirted houseman passed him, ignoring him. Pete toyed with his beer glass, joining the wet rings together on the bar top, and pondered the behavior of the two burly housemen. They both had appeared older than he, so was it protocol for him to go up to them and introduce himself? After all, each houseman's ultimate safety lay with the help the other four would give him if he got in a bind or was ganged. Could it be they were resentful that Maule, through Josh Eddy, had hired this complete stranger they had been chasing last night?

As Pete finished his beer, the fifth houseman came out of the corridor that led to the offices and Pete saw him halt and survey the slowly filling room. His glance touched Pete and slid away and then he moved over to the faro layout. That summed it up for Pete. They were ignoring him purposely.

Well, that's all right with me, Pete thought; he had alternately been hazed and ignored for his first year at the military academy. It was understandable that men in any profession, even this one, were jealous of their skills and required of a newcomer that he show these same skills before they respected him.

Now, pool cue tucked under his belt on the left side, he began to cruise the rapidly filling room as were the other housemen. The townsmen were beginning to drift out and the miners and teamsters to drift in. He supposed there would be little trouble till the bar patrons got a skinful.

Presently, Lace came in through the corridor door, followed by Hagerty and the case tender. Hagerty laid his shotgun in the slots cut for it in the arms of his high chair and then proceeded to light the pull-down lamp over the faro table and the bracket lamp behind Lace. She had changed to a white blouse with lace at its throat and already men were drifting away from the other faro layout to hers.

While the other tables were mostly empty, one of the housemen lit the lamps above them against the lowering dusk. Without anybody telling him to, Pete began to light the bracket lamps spotted on the wall at intervals. It was only a matter of minutes before the flood tide of miners jammed through the Crossfire doors. The din in the room swelled and now Pete began to cruise behind the men jammed three-deep at the bar. He met a houseman making the same cruise in the opposite direction and neither looked at the other.

The first trouble came just after dark and Pete was closest to it. Two mustachioed miners at the door end of the bar raised their voices in anger, speaking in a language Pete could not understand. They were squared off to fight when Pete moved in, put an arm under the arm of each of them and slowly, but steadily, marched them out of the door. Once on the dirt walk, they began their fight, which was such a clumsy affair that the passers-by did not bother to watch. When he turned back into the room, Pete noted that one of the housemen had watched the eviction from a distance, but had made no effort to help. Likely he spotted them as harmless, Pete reflected.

Remembering Josh Eddy's admonition of this afternoon, he moved through the press of the crowd toward Lace's faro layout.

He was close to it when Hagerty spotted him. A look of surprise washed over the mean old man's face and he started to raise his gun. Then he caught sight of Pete's white shirt and his jaw slacked open. He lowered the shotgun and his left hand beckoned Pete toward him.

Pete shoved through the crowd and halted before Hagerty's high chair.

"Ain't you the cowboy that started that fight last night?" At Pete's nod, Hagerty said in a truculent voice, "What are you doing in that white shirt?" He spoke so loudly that Lace heard him. Without taking her glance from the game, she said, "Forget it, old man. He works here."

Pete grinned at him and moved away, heading toward the bar again. Turned half-sideways, he thrust through the crowd and now became aware of the stink of this place. Tobacco smoke, the reek of whisky, garlic, and plug tobacco could not hide the sweaty stench of these unwashed bodies.

He shoved past a bearded miner as tall as he was and then felt his arm grabbed. He was turning when the man beside him lunged against his back, pinioning his arms. He was a powerful man, for Pete was lifted clear off the floor and swung around to face the huge, bearded miner.

Pete was clawing unsuccessfully for his pool cue when the big miner drove a looping blow aimed at his face. Pete turned his head and ducked it and the blow rocketed off his skull, throwing the miner off balance and into him. Pete lifted a knee into the miner's groin and heard a bellow of pain as the miner jackknifed over.

Again Pete lifted his knee, this time to the miner's bearded face. By now the crowd had made room for them and Pete looked down and saw the boots of the man who was holding his arms, his unshaven chin buried in the base of Pete's neck.

Pete lifted a leg and stomped down on one booted foot and heard the grunt of pain. He half-turned in his savage wrestle to free himself, and then, remembering that the bearded miner, bent over, was now behind him, he drove his heels into the floor and pushed himself and the man on him backward. The last thing he saw before he and the bear of a man on his back tripped over the bearded miner, was the white shirt of a houseman watching the brawl. He wasn't moving, he was watching.

The jarring fall broke the hold of the man who was pinioning him and now Pete, topmost on the three-man pile, rolled free and swiftly came to his feet facing his opponents.

The man who had pinioned him was a blocky, muscular miner, whose arms were so thick they had long since split both sleeves of his shirt. He was sprawled across the bearded miner, who on hands and knees was trying to buck the other's legs off his back. He succeeded, for the blocky miner rolled off and into the crowd and was getting up as Pete lunged toward the bearded miner.

Pete, his right hand clenched, brought his fist down on the base of the bearded miner's neck and wheeled away just as the blocky miner stepped over his fallen partner and charged.

Pete took a step back, reaching for the pool cue, and found that at some time in the struggle it had come loose from his belt.

He reached in his pocket for his knife, at the same time dodging the head-down charge of the blocky miner. He found the knife and folded it into his left palm so that its bulk would cushion his knuckles, and waited for the bulky miner.

He came in with his arms outstretched, and Pete knew the man was prepared to take any amount of punishment if he could get those huge arms around his opponent and squeeze the very life out of him, cracking countless ribs in the process. The man's body, toughened by years of swinging a single jack, would be, Pete knew, impervious to almost any blow.

Accordingly, Pete made his decision, a distasteful one. He would go for the head and probably smash some knuckles in the process. He made a second charge by driving his knife-clenched fist into the miner's nose and he felt it give. In the moment that the charge was stopped, he stepped back and away. The miner shook his head, his eyes watering, and then the blood began gushing from his nostrils.

Again the miner charged, arms spread for the hug, and again Pete stepped aside and drove a glancing blow that broke the skin on the miner's forehead. Patiently, paying it no attention, the miner continued his pursuit. Pete started a step to his right, and when he saw the miner anticipating it and trying to cut him off, Pete took a step to his own left and had a clear shot with a hook at the miner's left eye socket. It was a hurting blow to both men and Pete felt the shock of it clear up to his shoulder. The crowd was yelling now, pushing and contracting the circle they had cleared for the fight. Someone, Pete saw, had dragged the bearded miner out of the fight space.

Pete began a circle of the miner, who was now a little wary. Pete saw that the forehead gash was bleeding as well, for the miner was wiping blood out of his eyes. He was, of course, breathing through his mouth, for his mashed nose was still streaming blood. More slowly now, arms still outspread, he tried to close again with Pete and caught the knife-supported fist in his mouth. Again Pete drifted to his right just out of reach of the miner's huge arms. They circled each other warily for a moment. Pete saw his last blow had mashed the miner's lips and they too were bleeding. The front of the man's shirt was sodden with blood.

The miner made a sudden lunge. Pete backed up and was brought up short by the press of bodies. The miner caught Pete's forearm before Pete could dodge, but the blood on the miner's hands made his grip so slippery that Pete wrenched free. Now the miner halted, wiping the blood from his eyes and face with his forearm.

"Had enough?" Pete asked.

"Stand still and fight, damn you," the miner said through bloody lips.

"Come and get me," Pete taunted.

He moved to the right and the miner was so slow to react that Pete moved in a little and threw a right at the miner's left eye, then danced away. There was pandemonium in the room now. Miners had climbed up on the bar so they could get a better view. Among them was a white-shirted houseman.

Now the miner halted again, wiping at his eyes with raised forearm. Pete, knowing that his arm was blocking his sight, moved to the right and then drove his right fist to the side of the miner's jaw. The force of the blow staggered the man and his arm fell to his side. It was then that Pete moved in with a short right jab to the point of the miner's broad jaw. His head snapped back so his eyes were pointed at the ceiling; at the same time his knees came unhinged. He fell to the floor on his knees and made no attempt to check the heavy fall on his side, then slowly rolled over on his back like a tired child, his arms at his sides.

A great roar welled up from the crowd. A couple of watching miners who were standing on the bar started a fight, and a houseman standing on the bar pushed his way toward them, shoving anyone in his way off the bar.

There was one last chore Pete knew he had to attend to. He leaned down and picked up one of the miner's feet and then said to the group nearest him, "Give me a hand here, someone, will you?" A miner stepped forward and took the other leg and the crowd made way for them as they dragged the miner across the floor and out of the door. Once outside, they sat him up against the window.

Pete drew a coin from his pocket and said to the man who had helped him, "Buy yourself a beer, friend, and then bring two beers out here."

The man left with the money and Pete looked down at the blood-spattered miner whose head was cocked a little as if he were listening. There was something this man knew and was going to tell him, Pete thought grimly. In another minute the miner groaned and his head came up. His first act was to lean over and spit blood and then he wiped his face with the forearm of his blood-soaked shirt.

At last the miner lifted a knee in preparation to standing up.

Pete said, "Sit there a minute," and the knee came down. The man who had been sent for the beer now returned with a mug in each hand. Pete accepted the two beers and the man said, "You got some change comin'."

"Keep it," Pete said. "Thanks very much."

When the man disappeared into the saloon, Pete knelt by the miner. "Put out your hand. Here's a beer," he said.

Pete held out the beer but the man reached past him. Pete guessed that one or both of his eyes were swollen shut. He steered the beer to the miner's hand and then sat down beside him on the hard-packed earth under the coal-oil flare. The miner took his first sip, rinsed the blood out of his mouth and spat out the beer, then took a deep pull from the mug. Pete took a drink from his beer too. The two men sat there in contented silence until the miner, finishing his beer, said, "Ah, that's fine."

"What's your name, Irish?" Pete asked civilly.

"Murphy, it is."

"Murphy, who paid you and that big lad to jump me tonight?"

There was a long silence, and then Murphy turned his head toward Pete. "Nobody," he said.

Pete was silent a moment, listening to the din from inside. Then he said, "I guess the waltz isn't over, Murphy. You'd better stand up and we'll go at it again."

"Not tonight. Some other time."

"No, right now. I want to know who paid you and you're going to tell me."

"If I tell you, they'll beat me up, sure."

"If you don't tell me, I'll beat you up, sure, Murphy."

Murphy seemed to think this over and he said, "Will you keep them off me?"

"As long as you behave yourself in the Crossfire I will. Now who are they?"

"Three of them housemen. Shields, Becker and Burns. Ten dollars for Logan, ten dollars for me and all the booze we could drink. The fourth one, Petersen, didn't like it, but he said he wouldn't side with you." He added, almost irrelevantly. "You're a rough man, and I think you'll keep them off me."

"You have my word, Murphy."

Pete rose, took the glass from Murphy and said, "Can you make it to bed?"

"I'll sleep here a while and then try."

"Then good night, Murphy."

Pete entered the crowded saloon and put down the beer glasses at the end of the bar. He noticed for the first time that his knuckles were swollen, skinned and bloody and that his white shirt was spattered with blood. He headed down the bar, aiming for the washroom off the corridor. On both sides of him as he made his slow way, men slapped him on the shoulder and seemed to be telling him in a half-dozen languages that it had been a grand fight. The irony of it was not lost on Pete. He had beaten up two of their number, but they didn't seem to care or resent it. The spectacle of the fight had made the evening for them and they were thanking him, much as they would pat a dog who had won a spectacular fight in the street. On his way he didn't encounter any of the housemen.

In the filthy washroom with its one tap over a zinc basin, Pete bathed the blood off his hands and afterward moved down to Josh Eddy's office where a lamp was burning. Slowly, hands fumbling, he got out of his bloody shirt and shrugged into a fresh one, and all the while he was remembering what Murphy had told him. The fight had been arranged and paid for by the other four housemen, who had refused to break it up. The reason for this was lost on him. Had they done it to test him, or had they done it out of revenge for his handling of Micky Howard, one of their brotherhood? More important, was Josh Eddy in on their plans? But most important of all, did Ben Maule know of the plot? Maybe he had even suggested it as punishment for Pete's beating one of the housemen.

One thing he was certain of was that without the protection of the other housemen, he couldn't survive this job.

Their lack of any attempt to break up the fight or to protect him hadn't gone unnoticed by the Crossfire customers. It would be interpreted as an open invitation to gang him. The miners hated the housemen, and the rough treatment they had received from them would guarantee their reprisal against him, especially if the other housemen permitted it.

As he turned into the corridor to return to his job he had no answers to these questions.

He obtained another sawed-off pool cue from the same bartender and then cruised the crowd. That last half hour before midnight, the other housemen were careful to avoid him and he didn't seek them out. When midnight came, the housemen closed the card games and began to herd the miners out. Pete left that chore to them. He got his shirts and gun belt from Eddy's office and went out the back door.

Tramping down the alley, he couldn't see how his job, even if it continued, brought him any closer to accomplishing what he had been sent here to do—get Ben Maule to the nearest army post to be tried.

He turned into the walkway and past the dark window of Laurie's room. He walked carefully for he didn't want to awaken or alarm her.

As soon as he opened the door of the rooming house, he could look down the corridor and see that a lamp was burning in the kitchen. As he closed the door as softly as possible, he saw Laurie appear and halt in the kitchen doorway. There was enough light from the corridor lamp for him to see her beckoning gesture and he started down the corridor.

Laurie turned and disappeared from sight and when he reached the kitchen, he saw her seated in a chair at the round kitchen table under the bracket lamp on the wall. As he came up to her, he remembered the blood-spattered shirt trailing from his side pocket so that it would not soil the shirts he carried under his arm. It was too late to do anything about it now. As he halted and took off his hat, he said, "Why are you still up, Miss Laurie?"

"To see if you could make it up the stairs," Laurie said quietly.

Pete was silent a moment, watching her look at his skinned knuckles which were still oozing blood. "You heard, then?"

Laurie nodded. "All that shouting woke me and when Mr. Moynihan came in I asked him what it was all about. He told me about your fight." She rose now, tightened the belt on her blue wrapper and said, "Sit down, Pete, and we'll soak those hands. I have hot water ready, and I admit I was expecting worse."

Pete sat down while Laurie got a basin from the counter which held torn strips of white bandage. She put the bandages on the table and moved over to the stove and filled the basin with warm water. Afterward, she brought the basin back and said, "Let's look at your hands."

Pete held them out and Laurie, examining them, only shook her head. She tested the water with her hand and said, "Try it."

As Pete put his hands gingerly into the warm water, Laurie sat down.

"Mr. Moynihan said the other housemen didn't help you."

"It must have been their night off for breaking up fights," Pete said dryly.

"But why? That's what they're there for, isn't it, to beat up miners and protect each other?"

"Maybe they're remembering the night before."

Laurie picked up a bandage, soaked it in the pink water, and then gently washed the knuckles on both of Pete's hands. She bandaged them and then set the basin aside. "What are you going to do, Pete? The same thing could happen every night, couldn't it?"

"I'll know tomorrow," Pete said soberly. Then he smiled at her. "I can't say you didn't warn me."

"You just don't belong there," Laurie said with quiet vehemence.

"I belong anywhere I can make it stick," Pete said evenly. He rose. "Thanks for waiting up for me, Laurie." He hesitated. "I mean, Miss Laurie."

Laurie smiled. "You were right the first time, Pete. It's Laurie. Now take that bloody shirt out of your pocket and leave it. I'll have it washed tomorrow."

After exchanging good nights, she watched him leave the kitchen, his steps slowed by weariness. Then, she took the basin over to the sink and washed it out. She had told Pete that Moynihan had watched the fight, but she did not tell him everything Moynihan had told her about it. He had said that, by all rights, the beginning of the fight indicated Pete was shortly headed for a long stay in Doc Price's hospital. Instead, with his arms pinioned, he had managed to eliminate the biggest of his assailants. Once free, he had, in Moynihan's words, "cut the other man to ribbons." It was as savage a fight as Moynihan had ever seen and he wondered where Brisbin, whom he had only just met, had learned his "wizardy in the fine art of mayhem."

Moynihan was a printer for the *Banning Banner* and a bit of a poet, but what he had said impressed Laurie.

Where had Pete Brisbin learned his roughneck ways and under what circumstances? Come to that, what did she know about him? Only that he had been gentle and polite to her and that his speech indicated he was better educated than she, in spite of her training from one-time schoolmarm Aunt Martha. Where he came from and what he was doing here and what he wanted here was a total mystery. All she really knew for sure was she liked him and was fearful for him.

5

Pete slept late and next morning, missing breakfast, he managed to escape the house without alerting Laurie or her aunt. He ate at the same Mexican cafe he had been in yesterday and found that with both hands bandaged it was slow work. Afterward, he went to the feed stable and asked that his horse be saddled. While the Mexican hostler was saddling up, Pete idly inquired the whereabouts of the ranch owned by Ben Maule. He was told that the Circle M lay some six miles out of Banning and was about the same distance from the border.

Once in the saddle and under a cloudless sky, Pete headed south. The country around him seemed bare desert, and the rolling wasteland of rock and sand or of yucca and mesquite and sahvaro baked in the sun. Such bunch grass that grew was so sparse that it would take three hundred acres of this land to graze one cow. For the first hour Pete saw no life from the dusty road except an occasional jack rabbit and the vultures wheeling overhead.

When far ahead of him he saw dust that could only be raised by a team or riders, he left the road, heading west, and sought the protection of an oven-hot canyon. He didn't want any of Maule's men to spot him and report his presence in the vicinity.

When he cut back to the road, the dust cloud was behind him.

Presently, the country altered subtly. It was less barren, if still desert, and he began to spot cattle. They were rangy longhorns and spooked like deer when he came close. Again he left the road, for he knew that if cattle were here so was water, and where there was water there would be people.

In another half hour, following a ridge which was slowly petering out, he got a glimpse of pure green foliage far ahead of him and then, as he rode up to rimrock, he saw a valley ahead of him. Its fields were irrigated and almost directly below the rimrock lay the big adobe ranch house. Between it and the irrigated fields were the corrals and outbuildings and the horse pasture, where many head of horse were grazing. From the base of the rimrock a sizable creek flowed past the ranch house through the horse pasture, and into the distant fields.

This could only be Ben Maule's Circle M. To build it, Ben Maule would have had to buy out a half-dozen families and their water rights, and only Ben Maule, in this country, had that kind of money.

When Pete had had his look, he began the ride back to town, still staying clear of the road. He wanted to be back in time to show up for work. He was curious as to what Josh Eddy would say about last night. From his brief talk with Eddy yesterday, he was struck by the man's absolute candor, and he wondered if Eddy would be equally candid today.

Back in town, he put up his horse and, neckerchief over his face and mouth against the ever-present dust, he headed under the *portals* for the Crossfire.

The big saloon held only a couple dozen customers, and as Pete walked down past the bar, he nodded to the bartenders. Two of them nodded back sullenly and the others greeted him with pleasant smiles and nods. This told him nothing. If they noted his bandaged hands, they were all too polite to remark them. The faro layouts were idle.

The back door was open, so the corridor was lighted. One of Maule's bodyguards was stationed in the corridor back against the wall. As Pete approached, the man raised his hand and pointed his thumb in the direction of Josh Eddy's office.

The door was open and before Pete could knock, Eddy saw him and waved him in. Ahead of him, Pete saw both

Ben Maule and Lace seated in armchairs facing Eddy's desk.

At his entrance, both of them glanced at him. Lace nodded and smiled and Ben Maule gave him the briefest of nods.

"How do you feel, Pete?" Eddy asked.

As Pete removed his hat he said, "Why, like I've been in a fight, Josh."

"Sit down," Josh said and indicated the same straight-backed chair against the wall by his desk.

Pete sat down and Ben Maule said idly, "We were just talking about it."

Lace said, "I watched it from Hagerty's chair. It was quite a fight."

"What started it?" Maule asked.

Pete looked at him levelly. "Did you?"

Maule's broad face showed open surprise, then he scowled. "Why would I?"

"Because I gave Micky Howard a rough time. Could that be it?"

"No."

Pete looked at Josh Eddy. "Did you?"

"Like Ben said, why would I?"

"For the same reason."

"Again, like Ben said, no." He paused. "What is it you're saying, Pete?"

"I was wearing one of those white shirts you told me to buy. That was so if I got in trouble the other housemen could spot me and come to my help. I was supposed to do the same for them in their white shirts, right?"

"That's what I said."

"Well, they watched the fight," Pete said. "One of them even stood on the bar to get a better look."

Maule said, "Is that true, Josh?"

"I don't know, but I'll find out," Eddy said grimly.

"It's true," Lace said. "Not a one of them gave him any help."

"Why didn't you tell me that last night?" Maule said to Lace.

"You were asleep when I came in and I didn't want to wake you. You were gone when I woke up. When you picked me up this afternoon I wanted to tell it in front of Josh. Pete just beat me to it."

Maule said softly, almost as if to himself, "Well, I'll be damned. Not a one of them helped you, Pete?"

Now's the time, Pete thought and he said, "No. Three of them paid the two that jumped me ten dollars a piece and all the whisky they could hold. Petersen wouldn't ante up for the beating but he promised not to help me."

Maule frowned and asked skeptically, "Now how did you find that out?"

"From the miner that lasted longest."

"And why would he tell you?" Maule asked, still skeptical.

"I told him I'd keep the fight going until he did tell me."

"And why did you think that anybody paid the miners to jump you? The housemen get jumped all the time."

"And other housemen help them when they are jumped," Pete said dryly. "When no help came I figured they'd got the word from you or Josh to let it happen. Either that, or the housemen wanted it to happen and paid for it."

Maule was silent a long moment considering what Pete had said and the implications. However, it was Lace who spoke first. "Don't you read it, Ben?"

Maule looked at her in puzzlement and said, "Read what?"

"Are you running your housemen or are they running you?"

"They were only getting even for Howard. You can't really blame them," Maule said.

"That's not an answer to my question," Lace said.

"Why, I'm running them."

"Right out of the Crossfire, I hope," Lace said.

"But they're good at their jobs," Maule protested.

"And brave too," Lace said scornfully. "So brave they hired two miners to take up their fight. What happens if they don't like your next housemen? The same thing? If that isn't running you, what is?"

Maule's head was turned toward Lace so that Pete couldn't see the expression on his face. He could see Lace's face, however. It was composed and her glance was challenging.

Suddenly, laughter exploded from Maule. "By God, you're right, Lace." He turned his head to look at Eddy. "Pay off the lot of them, Josh."

"And tell them why?" Josh asked.

"You bet," Maule said crisply. To Pete he said, "You satisfied?"

"Can I say something before saying yes?" Pete asked.

"Go ahead."

Pete talked to Eddy now. "Josh, why not fire them on the grounds they didn't come to my help. Leave out that business of them paying the miners."

"All right, but why?"

"Because if they know you know it, it won't be a week before somebody finds those two miners dead in a back alley. They deserved the beating they got, but not a shot in the back."

"That's the way to do it, Josh, like he said," Maule said.

Eddy nodded, stood up, went over to the stubby safe whose door was already open, took out a buckskin sack of coins and left the room.

Pete rose now, hat in hand, and Maule said, "Sit a minute, Pete."

Pete reseated himself and Maule asked curiously, "You like your job?"

"No."

"Why is that?"

"Well, it's a necessary job, but if I liked doing this I'd probably have been some marshal's deputy or soldier a long time ago."

Maule nodded. "Maybe I can find something else for you. Let me think about it. All I can say is I'd like to keep you with me." He rubbed his square jaw and said, "Don't you work tonight. Come around tomorrow in the middle of the morning. I may have some news for you."

Pete nodded, rose, said goodbye to them both and went out. Glancing past the lookout in the corridor through the open door to Maule's office, he saw the other three bodyguards lounging there, one of them seated behind Maule's desk. Instead of heading out of the back door, he turned into the saloon. What Maule had just said about a change of jobs set in motion something he was going to do eventually anyway; this just pushed the time up. At the bar he bought a quart of whisky which the bartender, observing Pete trying to tuck it in his jacket pocket, took back and thoughtfully wrapped in a newspaper.

Pete sought the street now, and headed up it to the cross street which was quieter and not so dusty. As he tramped up it, he thought of the four-way conversation that had just taken place in Josh Eddy's office. For some reason it depressed him, when it should have filled him with a mild elation. Hadn't Ben Maule first saved him from the beating yesterday, and today, under Lace's gentle prodding, ordered Eddy to fire the housemen? Hadn't Josh been willing to keep silent on the bribery charge in order to protect Murphy and Logan? And to cap it all, hadn't Ben Maule promised him a different job, because he wanted him with him? They had all treated him fairly and with friendliness and, so help him, he was beginning to like them. Orders, of course, were orders, but what if the company clerk had been wrong in his identification? What if he himself was repaying loyalty with treachery, only to find that Maule was the wrong man?

Sure, there were some unsavory things about Maule. He was living with a woman he was not married to, but hadn't man been doing that since Adam? True, Maule surrounded himself with hardcases, but all strong men through history had done the same. He had corrupted the law, but even in politics what strong man hadn't? What he wanted to know specifically that Laurie couldn't tell him, was what Maule had done that would justify what Horton's company clerk had written. Any man who would lead a massacre of a paymaster's detail wouldn't vary that pattern of violence. If Pete could learn of other crimes he had committed, his conscience would stop nagging him. He intended to do just that tonight.

Crossing the alley, the sight of the frame bathhouse abutting the alley reminded Pete that if he was to get a shower before supper, he would have to hustle.

When Pete was well out of hearing, Maule rose, circled the desk, and sat down in Josh Eddy's chair where he could see Lace better.

"What do you think, Lace?" he asked.

"Of him?"

"No, of keeping him with me."

Lace shrugged. "Do you need him? And how would you use him?"

"I just hate to pass him up. The way he came back and asked me for a job took more guts than I've got. Tell me about last night's fight."

"I don't know much about fights," Lace said, and added thoughtfully, "All I know is that he went at it for keeps."

There were voices now in the corridor outside, and a man who seemed to have entered from the alley halted in the doorway. He was taller than Maule but not so wide, maybe forty and wearing clean range clothes. Pinned on the left of his double-breasted shirt was the star of the sheriff's office. His features were swarthy, his high-bridged nose aquiline, falsely suggesting Indian blood, for his mother was an Iowa Smith and his father a Texas Collier.

"Want to talk with you, Ben, when you've got a minute."

Lace rose and said, "I'll see you later, Ben. How are you, Collie?"

"Hot, like everybody, Lace."

Lace moved past him and headed for the saloon, and Maule rose. "Let's go over to my office, Collie. It's a little cooler there."

Maule led the way to the office across the way and on entering, said to his bodyguard, "You boys leave us alone."

They rose, greeted the sheriff with familiarity, and stepped out into the corridor. The sheriff, who was one of three deputies in this vast county, closed the door, shoved his Stetson back on his head, and moved over to the armchair facing the desk. When he had seated himself, Maule said, "Got something on your mind, Collie? Besides money, I mean."

They both laughed. Deputy Sheriff Collier's broad smile revealed white unstained teeth which made him seem a little less fierce-looking. "No, it's still money," he said.

"Let's hear it."

"Well, we been around and around on this before, Ben, but I think you ought to think about it again."

"I can guess," Maule said. "Your girls."

The sheriff nodded. "They're not making me the money they should, Ben, and you know why. They got no place to meet the men except those damn cribs. If you'd let them in here where the boys could see them, they'd double their take."

Maule said patiently, "Collie, we been through this a dozen times. There's only one woman I want in here, and that's Lace. You run the whores and I'll run the games and booze."

"But they go together," the sheriff said. "Together, we double our take."

Maule shook his head. "Build yourself a house, Collie, and bring out a madam from San Francisco."

"No, if I had that kind of money I'd build me a saloon with the girls upstairs." He looked challengingly at Maule.

"Would you, now?" Maule asked softly.

"Want to throw in with me on it?"

Maule looked at him levelly and the sheriff's gaze held

his. Maule said then, a faint chill in his voice, "You sound as if you had plans, Collie."

The sheriff nodded. "I have." Again the two men regarded each other in silence. Maule said quietly, "That wasn't our deal. Outside of the hotel I was to have the only booze in town."

"Times change, Ben and . . ."

"No, they don't," Maule interrupted.

The sheriff leaned forward in his chair and said angrily, "Look, I'm giving you a chance to throw in with me half and half on a saloon with girls. We couldn't help but make money, Ben." Then he added, "What the hell's got into you —religion?"

"You're the one that's changed, Collie. I haven't."

"What've you got against women, Ben? You're living with one whenever you want to. Other men have got to have 'em. Why not make money off them?"

Before the sheriff had finished, he knew he had made a mistake. Although not intending it, he had made it sound as if he put Lace in a class with the whores.

Maule's face went white with anger. Without saying anything, he rose, moved around the desk, skirted the sheriff in his chair and opened the corridor door. He called then, "Come in, boys." His four bodyguards, who had been just outside the door, filed into the room.

The sheriff, more puzzled than alarmed, was rising as Maule said, "Put a gun on him, Lefty."

Swiftly, Lefty covered the sheriff. It was done so quickly that Collier didn't have time to lift his hand toward his gun. Without having to be told, Lefty moved over to the sheriff and lifted the gun from his holster. Maule said then, "Throw that pimp out in the street. Make sure a lot of people see you do it."

The bodyguards were on the sheriff instantly, one to each arm. The third bodyguard grabbed the sheriff's belt in back. It was too late to struggle to any effect but Collier tried. With his arms pinned up behind his back, he was helpless.

With a man behind lifting him so that the toes of his boots barely touched the floor, the three men propelled him out of the door, down the corridor, and into the barroom that was just beginning to fill up. By the time they had passed the bar, knocking customers aside, they were at a trot. When they hit the open doors, all three of the men heaved the sheriff's body.

Off balance, his legs trying to catch up with his momentum, Collier staggered and stumbled and finally crashed into the tie rail, which caught him across the midriff. He tried to grab the rail but failed, slid over and pitched headlong, face down, into the deep dust of the street. As a final act of humiliation, his gun came sailing across the tie rail and landed in the dust beside him.

Back in the office, Maule sat down in his chair again, feeling the pulse of anger hammering in his temples. When it subsided a little, he tried to assess the consequences of this quarrel. They would be negligible, he knew. Collier was only one man against his own large crew and official help was four days away. But he wouldn't send for it, Maule knew. If he did, all Maule would have to do would be to say that this law-enforcing deputy was running a string of girls who turned over half their earnings to him. Once that was known, Collier would be just another saddle tramp looking for work. No, Collier would keep his mouth shut and accept his humiliation.

Still, the very proposition Collier presented to him held a threat. It would be easy enough for Collier to find other sources of secret money to build his own saloon and bring his girls into a more attractive setting. With any kind of financial backing, he could match hardcase for hardcase with Maule. That, Maule knew, must be prevented at all costs.

6

Pete had his shower, changed socks and shirt and climbed the back stairs to his room. When he entered it, he found that in his absence his freshly washed and repaired shirt had been laid on the bed along with some fresh bandages. He was putting on the bandages when the supper bell rang. He managed to tie the bandages by holding the strings with his teeth, but it took him so long that he was the last one at the table. His housemates greeted him civilly and looked at his bandaged hands with such curious respect that they might have been war wounds. All the heaping dishes came at him from both sides. He was about to help himself when Laurie, whom he had not even seen, reached over his shoulder and heaped his plate with the food that had been passed.

"Why don't you wait for me to tie those?" Laurie said, half-scolding. She was wearing her gray uniform dress and Pete wondered what she would look like in something less drab.

"It was easy," Pete said. "I tied them with my toes."

Laurie smiled, poured his coffee and went back into the kitchen.

There was little conversation at the table and what there was Pete couldn't understand. He kept glancing at Moynihan across the table. He was a sallow, gangling man who never managed to get his bony hands scrubbed clean of the printer's ink. A man of forty-five with only a saddle of hair across his balding head, he had a taciturnity about him that, when broken, erupted in wry observations that usually brought smiles from his listeners.

Pete had started supper so late and it was such slow eating with his bandaged hands that the others were finished before him. Singly or in pairs they left the dining room. Moynihan was the last of them to leave and as he passed behind Pete's chair he halted.

"They give you a night off, eh?" he asked.

Pete looked up at him and held up his hands. "I'm not much good to them with these."

Moynihan grinned, revealing oversized tobacco-stained teeth. "Ask me, they should give you a week off and with pay too." He paused as if uncertain and then asked, "Why didn't them other housemen help you?"

"It's a long story," Pete said. "Where can I find you later?"

"Well, I had a little poker in mind at the hotel, but that can wait."

"No, go ahead. I'll see you there later."

Moynihan nodded and left just as Laurie came in with a tray to start clearing the tables.

"Like your supper?" Laurie asked.

"If you're fishing for a compliment, you don't have to. I can't remember a better one."

Laurie smiled with pleasure, then said, "You're not supposed to be here at this hour. Are you fired?"

Pete rose. "Let's get the dishes in the kitchen and I'll tell you about it." Together they quickly cleared the two tables. Aunt Martha and the Mexican woman were attacking the dishes at the sink and Pete thought Aunt Martha's nod to him was just barely civil. He knew that she disapproved of his job and even more of last night's fight.

Once Laurie had wiped the tables, she brought in a lighted lamp from the kitchen and they took chairs side by side at the farthest of the two round tables. Laurie listened to his account of the meeting in Josh Eddy's office with an expression of growing disbelief on her face.

When he had finished, Laurie was silent, almost brooding, then she said, "He must like you, Pete. That means you better be careful."

"The trouble is I'm beginning to like him too."

"Do you like what he does?" Laurie asked.

"I'm not sure I know anything he does except own a rough saloon, some business property, a mine and a ranch. I'm going to try to find out more about him tonight."

"Who'll tell you, Pete?"

"If I can get Moynihan to talk, I think he'd know. Every newspaper office I've ever known anything about was sitting on stories they won't or can't print, or are afraid to. Who owns the *Banner*?"

Laurie smiled. "Ames Williams is the editor, but Ben Maule's money is behind it."

"So it's no use talking to him."

"Is it any more use talking to Moynihan?"

Pete frowned. "I'd guess there is, Laurie. I think he probably knows as much about Maule as Williams, and he's got no stake in the *Banner*."

"Only his job," Laurie pointed out.

"That never bothers a printer, or any that I've known. If they aren't fired after six months of working, then they'll quit. They're a fiddle-footed breed and they like the drink, as the Irish say. That's what I'm counting on."

Laurie frowned now. "You mean you're going to get him drunk?"

"If I have to. I'll see that he makes it to his room."

Laurie pondered this and then gave a little sigh. "Well, I guess it doesn't matter who gets him drunk. He'll get himself drunk anyway."

"Can I borrow another glass from the kitchen, Laurie?"

Laurie smiled and said, "For that foul purpose, I guess you can."

When she returned with a glass, Pete was standing. She turned it over to him and said soberly, "Whatever you learn from him, Pete, be careful how you use it."

"We'll decide that between us, Laurie. Is that a deal?"

"Yes. Oh, very much a deal." The relief in her voice did not escape Pete. He said good night, took the glass up to his room and lighted the lamp, put on his jacket against the coming of the night chill, and left the house.

Pete found Moynihan in the small bar of the hotel. It was a low-ceilinged room that held two card tables, only one of which was being used. A pair of townsmen were at the end of the short bar behind which was a Mexican bartender. When Pete walked up to the bar, Moynihan saw him, cashed in his chips, rose and, carrying an empty glass, joined him.

Pete told the bartender to give Moynihan whatever he was drinking, ordered a beer for himself and then said to Moynihan, "You still want to hear my long story?"

When Moynihan said he sure as hell did, Pete started out with the trouble he'd got in at the Crossfire the night he arrived in town. He explained how he had met Laurie and how she had scolded away his pursuers.

"That's like her," Moynihan said. "She's a sweet girl to anybody she likes."

Pete agreed on that and went on to tell of his meeting with the hardcases and Ben Maule next morning. A look of pure appreciation came into Moynihan's face as Pete described what happened there. By the time he'd got this far, Moynihan's drink was down and Pete's beer was drunk. Moynihan ordered another round. Pete went on then, describing Eddy's instructions as to his duties. He told of being jumped later in the evening by the two miners and of the housemen's refusal to help him. He omitted Murphy's story of the housemen paying them to beat up the new houseman. He picked up the story where he had confronted Maule and Eddy this afternoon. His account of the conversation was reorganized a little so as to make Maule seem more indignant than he really had been about the housemen's failure to come to his help. By the time he reached Maule's decision to fire the housemen and Eddy paying them off, his beer was gone and Moynihan's glass empty.

"What a story," Moynihan said thoughtfully. "Except it don't sound like Maule."

"That's the way it happened." Then, as if just remembering, he said, "Say, I've got a bottle back in my room. Why don't we go work on it while you give me some advice?"

"Whisky?" Moynihan asked. When Pete nodded, Moynihan said, "I'm your man. Let's go."

As they stepped out of the street door, Moynihan leading, he stopped and looked at the building across the street where there was a lamp lighted behind the barred windows. When Pete hauled up beside him, Moynihan looked at him with a grin.

"Hear about the dust-up this afternoon?"

When Pete said he had not, Moynihan started walking and Pete fell in alongside him. "They tell me Sheriff Collier got thrown out of the Crossfire this afternoon. Maule's boys gave him the running heave over the tie rail, and he lit flat on his face."

"What was all that about? I thought the sheriff was Maule's man."

"Always has been," Moynihan said cheerfully.

They were at Main Street now and Moynihan said, "Let's go a block over and get out of this dust." As they crossed the street between the high-wheeled ore wagons, one of whose lead team had a lighted lantern fastened to its collar, Moynihan cursed the dust. Once across the street and headed down the side street, Moynihan explained that the forbiddingly high cost of water here ruled out keeping Main Street watered down. Pete was only half-listening for he was still wondering what had provoked Maule to throw the sheriff out of the Crossfire. When Moynihan fell silent, Pete said, "What favors did Maule and Collier trade, Moynihan?"

"Why, the sheriff lets Maule's hardcases wreck any new saloons that start up. Maule lets Collier shake down all the whores in the North end cribs. What I mean is, he doesn't bring in any girls himself to compete with Collier." Moynihan looked now at Pete and grinned again. "I suppose you'd call that a gentlemen's agreement—if they were gentlemen."

"What do you think was behind that toss-out at the Crossfire?"

"Money," Moynihan said briefly, and to the point.

Upstairs at the rooming house, Moynihan stopped at his own room long enough to pick up a chair which he carried down to Pete's room. There, with the ever-cooling night breeze nudging the curtain of the open window, the two men sat facing each other across the washstand, whose pitcher and bowl Pete put on the floor beside him. The bottle, the lamp, and the two filled glasses rested on the washstand.

Moynihan, who seemed to Pete to be carrying his liquor well, took a deep drink and then asked, "What's troubling you, my friend, that you need advice from me?"

Pete was silent a moment and then said, "I guess you'd say it's Ben Maule. I told you he wants to keep me, but do I want to keep him?"

Moynihan, his dark eyes bright with liquor, appraised him shrewdly.

Pete went on, "I know the surface things about him, but you know more. If he owns the paper, then there are things your editor knows about him that he can't print. What are they?"

"Stay away from him," Moynihan said enigmatically.

"Why should I? That's what I want to know."

"Well, they tell me he came in this camp leading six men, all hardcases. He was a hardcase too, make no mistake about that. He looked around until he found that green valley where his Circle M is. There were six or seven Mexican families farming there." He took a sip of his drink. "He took that valley just the way the *ricos* took land in Mexico a hundred years ago. First he destroyed their crops, then, by God, he laid siege to their dobes, one by one. He'd attack a place at night and he never left a survivor, man, woman or

child. After the third massacre, the rest of those poor igno-
rant Mexicans pulled stakes and went back to Mexico."

"What about the law?"

"What law there was was busy with claim jumpers and
shootings. Hell, nobody knew those Mexicans existed. I
don't reckon the Mexicans even knew they were in the U.S.
They just ran, and Maule took over their land."

"How did he get his mine?"

"There were two brothers had some claims but they were
strapped. For enough money to get them started Maule got
a fiftieth share. Five days later his men picked a fight with
the two brothers and killed them. Maule showed the recorder his written agreement with the boys. As part-owner
he was entitled to the claims, he said. He likely bribed the
recorder, because the recorder agreed with him."

"Didn't the brothers have any family?" Pete asked.

"Who knows. Even today, do I know if you've got a family? Do you know if I have one? When this camp started it
was filled with men that had only faces and names. They
had no history. If you could hold what you staked out, fine.
If you couldn't, nobody even remembered you, because
what was there to remember?"

Pete nodded. "I can see that." He sipped at his drink and
they were both silent for a moment. Then Pete said, "Maule
must have had some money when he rode in here."

"He did, when other men didn't. He had money to buy
powder and tools and hire miners. They told me he even
loaned out money at a murderin' interest, takin' claims as
collateral."

Pete said mildly, "But those are just things you heard,
Moynihan. What do you really know about him that's happened since you've been here?"

Moynihan finished his drink and helped himself to another from the bottle on the table. Pete reached down and
put the water pitcher on the table, but Moynihan only shook
his head.

After sipping his drink, Moynihan said, "Well, there's a

sealed letter of Maule's in our safe at the paper. It's addressed to the chief of police in San Francisco. The boss has orders to mail it when Maule gives the word. Maule even told him what was in it. It tells where the police can find Lace Ferrill."

"Why do they want her?"

"She was a partner in a confidence game that milked a lot of money from a San Francisco shipowner. That's why Lace is his girl and will stay his girl. If she gets any fool ideas, out the letter goes."

"That's only a way to hold a woman. Not a very nice way, but it's no crime," Pete said.

"Would you call gunrunning a crime?" Moynihan asked. "He's run enough over into Mexico to outfit an army."

Pete was silent. He was certain now that Ben Maule was Sergeant Fairly. The fact that he had come into this camp with money and men was suspicious in itself. The massacre of the Mexicans, while not proven, indicated that the man who helped murder the paymaster's detail wouldn't stop at the murder of a few Mexicans. The murder of the two brothers and the claim jumping was in the same pattern. Maule simply took by force or guile anything he wanted, which after all was what Sergeant Fairly did on that trail to Camp Stambaugh.

While Pete was thinking this, Moynihan finished off his glass of whisky and shuddered. Watching him, Pete guessed that counting the drinks he had probably had earlier in the evening and the ones Pete had seen him drink, Moynihan had put away better than a pint of whisky this evening. He asked, "Anything else?"

"I could go on all night. Hell, I have gone on all night. I got to get some sleep." He rose unsteadily to his feet, grabbing the back of the chair to keep himself upright. Pete rose too. "You go ahead, I'll bring your chair."

"No, I need it for a crutch," Moynihan said.

Pete moved around him and opened the door and watched as Moynihan, skidding the chair in front of him as support, lurched across the room and out of the door. In the corridor he stopped and peered drunkenly at Pete. "All I say is, keep away from him, my friend."

"Thanks, Moynihan, I'll think about that. Good night."

Pete watched Moynihan from the doorway till he finally made his room and disappeared into it. Then he closed the door, stretched out on the bed and stared at the ceiling.

Moynihan had told him enough rumour and fact that there was no doubt in his mind that he was dealing with a wickedly dangerous man. More than that, Maule had surrounded himself by men of the same breed who were just as dangerous if not as bright.

How was he going to pry Maule loose from his men, who were very likely some of the same men who had ambushed the paymaster's detail with him seven years ago? He didn't know if the fact that Maule wanted to keep him guaranteed that Maule would keep him close to him. Maule might stake him out at the Circle M or some place even more remote. Well, tomorrow would tell.

7

Pete showed up at Maule's office promptly at ten on the following fine sunny morning. Maule did not have to tell any of his bodyguards to lift Pete's gun. One did, then the bodyguards were told to wait in the corridor and to close the door after them.

Twenty minutes later, Pete left Maule's office with a job, one thousand dollars in banknotes and an errand to run. He retrieved his gun from the guard, crossed the dusty street, turned up the side street and entered the sheriff's office across from the hotel. He stepped into a small room holding a rolltop desk, gunrack and two chairs, one of them swivel. The door to the cell block behind the office was open and the cells empty.

Sheriff Collier, seated at the desk, heard his entrance and looked over his shoulder in annoyance.

"Morning, Sheriff," Pete said politely.

"Morning. What can I do for you?"

"Like to talk with you, if you've got a few minutes."

Collier's dark glance fell to Pete's hands and he said coldly, "You work at the Crossfire, don't you?"

"Did, one day. I'm fired."

Now Collier half-turned his chair and regarded Pete appraisingly. "Yes, I can spare you a minute. What's on your mind?"

Without being invited, Pete moved over to the straight chair beside the desk and sat down. His seeming boldness brought a scowl to Collier's face and he waited until Pete was seated before he said, "Maule send you?"

Pete frowned. "No, nobody sent me. Why would they?"

"I don't know, but why are you here?"

Pete stretched out his legs, crossed them at the ankles and thumbed his hat off his forehead. "Why, to ask some questions, I reckon. That all right?"

"Depends on what they are," Collier said indifferently.

"All right. First night I got here I went into the Crossfire—no women, except the faro dealer. One day and night I worked there before I was fired—no women. How come that?"

"Why don't you ask Maule?"

"I don't know Maule that well. I asked Eddy. He said it was a house rule. Show 'em out if they come in, he told me."

Collier snorted derisively. "If you're looking for a woman there's a row of cribs at the North end of town."

Pete grimaced. "I've seen 'em. No thanks. No, I'm not looking for a woman, I'm looking for a way to make money in this town."

"You and everybody else," Collier said dryly. "Got any ideas?"

"Yes, one. Only I don't know the ropes here. Maybe you can put me straight." He paused. "Why hasn't somebody opened up a saloon with a dance hall and girls upstairs? Not a fancy one, but a good one with honest card games. Now, if a man wants any fun here, he can go to sleep over his drink at the hotel, or he can go into that bear pit at the Crossfire where he has to breathe through his mouth against the stink. Or he can go to one of those North End cribs where the bed's still warm."

"It's Maule's town," Collier said coldly. "If anybody builds a place, his men wreck it."

"He'd never wreck mine," Pete said quietly. Then he asked blandly, "Why do you let him?"

Collier's already swarthy face grew darker. "Look, I'm just one man. He can round up twenty. I don't like those odds."

"What if somebody else does?" Pete asked quietly. "What would you do?"

"Like you, you mean?"

"Like me."

"Why, I'd see that you got a decent burial, I reckon."

"Nothing else? Nothing like throwing in with me?"

Collier straightened up in his chair and started to speak, but Pete raised a hand, palm out, to check him. "I think I know what you're going to say, Sheriff. It wouldn't look right for a sheriff to be part owner of a saloon and a house. Still, I could name you a dozen towns east and north of here that have got saloons owned by sheriffs or deputy sheriffs. It's a business like any other business, and here you won't have any preachers on your back. What's against it?"

Collier slowly settled back in his chair. He was looking at Pete, but not seeing him. He was thinking this over, Pete knew, and very carefully. Then he smiled and shook his head. "What do you take me for, fella? I don't even know your name. I . . ."

"The name's Pete Brisbin," Pete interrupted.

"All right, Brisbin. I was just going to say if you're talking about money I haven't seen the color of it."

Pete reached in his shirt pocket and pulled out a wad of bills tied by string and pitched it on the desk in front of Collier, saying, "Thousand dollars. All in fifties."

"Eastern money," Collier scoffed.

"But money just the same. I'll see that it's turned into gold, so don't worry about that." He paused. "Can you match it?"

Collier nodded. "And more." He got up, picked up the wad of bills and handed it back to Pete, then made a slow deliberate circle of the room, his glance on the floor. If Collier had any suspicions that he was an emissary of Maule's, the paper money helped to dispel them, for the bills which Maule had somehow contrived to round up were almost unknown in this camp.

Collier halted abruptly and turned his head to look at Pete. "How'd you happen to come to me? Who sent you?"

"I thought you'd know that, Sheriff. You've got the reason right there—Sheriff."

Collier only grunted and resumed his pacing. Pete said then, "After you swear me in as a deputy sheriff, that will be just twice the law for Maule to buck."

That stopped Collier and he looked at Pete in amazement. "You a deputy? Why, I'm only a deputy."

"If there's an emergency, you can swear in other deputies, can't you?"

"Where's the emergency?"

"Make one up."

"They'd never pay you."

"Who needs pay if he's got a saloon?"

Again Collier started prowling and then asked abruptly, "You any good with a gun?"

"Too good. Why do you think I'm in this God-forgotten camp?"

"You wanted?"

"Not under this name, Sheriff. Don't worry."

Collier came back to his desk and sat down. He sighed and shook his head. "This is too quick, Pete. But let me think it over."

Pete smiled faintly. "When you've thought it over, what do you think you'll say?"

Collier smiled too. "I think I'll say yes. But not now."

Pete rose now. "I'll be back tomorrow, Sheriff. Or if you make up your mind before that time, leave word with Laurie Mays at the boarding house. Just tell her you said yes."

It was Sheriff Collier who extended his hand first. Pete shook it and left.

Once on the dusty walk, Pete wondered how convincing he had been. Collier couldn't help but harbor the dregs of a suspicion that Maule had sent him, and it would not do to return to the Crossfire immediately. At the corner while he waited for a load of freight to pass, he looked back toward the sheriff's office to see if Collier was following him. The sheriff was not on this side of the street but he could have crossed it while Pete was approaching the corner. Pete looked across the street, and among the dozen or so people on their way to and from the hotel, he saw a figure that seemed vaguely familiar. The man was dressed in worn range clothes and a dusty black Stetson.

As Pete threaded his way through the traffic of the dusty road, he tried to place him. It must be a Crossfire customer, he thought, because almost the only men he had seen in this town, outside of his fellow lodgers, he had seen in the Crossfire.

Then it came to him. This was the burly and nameless Crossfire houseman who had watched the fight from a vantage point atop the Crossfire bar.

Pete crossed the street and kept on down the side street. The houseman paralleled him, occasionally glancing at him. Pete wished now he had asked Josh Eddy what he had said to the housemen when he fired them. Crossing the alley, Pete moved up toward the corner and then, because there was little traffic on the side street, he stepped out into the road to cut for the opposite corner. He and the houseman were on converging paths.

Pete slowed his pace and so did the houseman. Then, in order to cross for an oncoming team, Pete hurried his pace and so did the houseman. They were perhaps fifteen feet apart, when the houseman called roughly, "You!"

Pete turned his head and looked directly at him, then slowed down and halted. The houseman had halted too. He was a burly man with no neck and a fight-scarred, pock-marked face. Now he was standing with his feet spread a little, thumbs hooked in his shell belt, and teetering faintly, rocking heel and toe in the dust.

Pete said quietly, "I've seen you at the Crossfire."

"But not any more, you crybaby bastard."

Pete said, still mildly, "So you had to get drunk to brace me."

"Drunk or sober, it's here now."

Pete wondered fleetingly, and with a touch of fear, if he was up against a professional gunman. There was only one way to find out. He turned slightly so that his right side was to the houseman in order to diminish the size of the target he presented. He said then, "Not as long as you keep talking."

Pete was watching the houseman's hands when they lifted from his belt. Pete's right hand lifted too. In one flowing motion his gun came out and up, and because there was no time to sight, he swiveled his wrist and shot from the hip.

The houseman's gun had just cleared its holster when the slug from Pete's gun caught him in the chest. In reflex the houseman fired his gun into the ground as he was falling over backward. Slowly, Pete walked over and looked down at the houseman spread-eagled on his back. The houseman's head turned so that his right cheek was in the dust. Then he gave one rattling sigh and was still.

Pete stood over him, feeling both an anger and regret at the senselessness of the man's death.

The crowd began to gather, running from Main Street and attracted by the shots. In moments, Sheriff Collier broke through the small crowd. At the sight of Pete, a look of astonishment came into his face, only to be replaced by a scowl. He came over to the houseman, knelt, found no pulse in the thick wrist and stood up. "What happened?" he asked Pete.

"He followed me from across the street when I came out of your office. He braced me here," Pete answered.

"I know you have money on you, but how did he?"

"It wasn't that. He thought I cost him his job in the Crossfire."

"Yeah, I heard about that."

The sheriff turned to the crowd. "Anybody see it? Speak up."

"I did," a man said. "That dead one, he stopped the other. I couldn't hear what they was saying, but the dead one went for his gun first, but the other was faster. That's all."

"Anybody else see it?" the sheriff asked.

"I did, Collie," a man called from the outer fringe of the crowd. "It's just like he says."

The sheriff nodded and called to the man who had just spoken. "Barney, there's a stretcher just inside the cell block. Will you get it for me?"

The sheriff turned to Pete now and, with a nod of his head toward the dead man, said, "Three other housemen were fired along with him. If they feel like he does, you better watch out."

"I think so too," Pete said. "You holding me for anything?"

The sheriff smiled faintly. "You don't hold a man for killing in self-defense. Run along." As the crowd split to let Pete through, the sheriff called, "All right, move along, folks."

Pete went down the side street and when he came to the boarding house, he chose an empty chair under the *portal* that served as its veranda. He would have to wait until the crowd cleared off the side street and the houseman's body was carried off before attempting to see Maule. His impulse was to go inside and explain to Laurie what had happened. On second thought, what was there to explain, except that he had been braced and defended himself. She'd hear it from one of the boarders at the noon meal anyway.

As he sat there, a gray depression riding him, he thought of the unlikely succession of events that he had participated in, or had been forced on him since coming to Banning. All of them seemed to conspire against or confuse the purpose of his main job, which was to bring Maule to justice. Was he any closer to accomplishing that than he'd been the night he got in? Only a little closer, he judged.

The killing of a few minutes ago was no part of his plan; unless I might say my plan for survival, he thought wryly. True, he was inching his way into Maule's confidence, but that was the only plus mark he had scored in four days. Except, of course, meeting Laurie. Even the relationship with her was becoming precarious, and Aunt Martha would see to it that it became even more so. He longed to tell Laurie his mission here, which might explain to her the truculence which he was required to show to the town. He knew he could trust her with his secret, but in defending him against Aunt Martha, she might inadvertently give away something that might endanger the success of his mission.

Judging that the crowd had had time to disperse, he rose now and took the walkway back to the alley and, seeing it empty, entered the open rear door of the Crossfire. The bodyguards were standing in the corridor, which meant Maule was talking privately with someone in his office. One guard lifted Pete's gun and Pete said to another of the guards, Lefty, "Tell him I'm here."

"Sure," Lefty said and then added, "That musta been a close one out there."

"They're all close," Pete said and turned into Eddy's office, which was empty. He sat down in the armchair facing the desk, thinking that if Lefty knew about the street fight, Maule would know too.

He was wondering what Maule's reaction to the news would be, when Maule himself, his calico shirt drenched with sweat from the heat of the closed room he had just left, came in. He gave Pete a brief look and a smile and seated himself in the chair behind Eddy's desk.

"They tell me Larry Burns jumped you."

"Was that his name? I never knew which was which."

Maule nodded. "Well, you only beat some miner to it." He leaned forward. "Tell me about Collie."

Pete told him everything that was said at his meeting with the sheriff. As he finished, he took out the folded bills and tossed them on the desk in front of Maule, who frowned as he put them in the desk drawer.

"Sounds to me like he's going to take you up on your new saloon. Did it to you?"

"Yes."

Maule rose. "Come along, Pete."

Pete followed him into the office across the corridor where three men were seated in chairs facing Maule's desk, talking in low voices. At Maule's entrance, talk stopped and the men rose. At first glance Pete judged two of them were townsmen, whose work kept them out of the sun. One, while he was dressed in rough clothes, didn't look a workman. Pete guessed by the muddy boots that he was probably connected with a mine.

Maule said, his finger poised for identification, "No hand-shaking boys, Pete's got a busted fist." Then the finger fell, pointing to the miner. "Pete, this is Tom Chapman from the Consolidated." His finger moved to the middle man. "Otey Collins, he runs my store for me." It wasn't necessary to point to the last man and his hand dropped. "Bill French, treasurer of the Lucky Lady." To them he said, "This is our Pete Brisbin."

All three nodded and Pete nodded back. "These gentlemen are our town council, Pete. The mayor would be here but he's out prospecting. He's outvoted though, any way you look at it."

The three councilmen smiled and Maule continued speaking to Pete. "We've just been going over the townsite charter. The council has the power to appoint a marshal. When the county gave up a deputy, we figured we didn't need a marshal, so we fired the one we had. Now we do need one. If you'll accept the job, Pete, you're the new marshal."

Pete looked at the group in puzzlement. "Why, I've only been here four days."

"All the better," Maule said. "If you don't know anyone you won't play favorites."

Without waiting for Pete to protest further, Maule said to the councilmen, "You give Pete a little time, and I'll give him a little talk. Thank you for your time, boys."

It was a dismissal and all three men nodded their goodbyes and left the room.

"Sit down, Pete."

Pete seated himself in one of the chairs and Maule eased into his own behind the desk.

"They can't be serious, can they?" Pete said.

"Sure, because I'm serious. One of them owes me his living, the other two owe me favors."

"In other words, you want your own marshal?"

"Why, how else can I fight this new saloon Collie wants to set up?"

"What can a marshal do about that?"

"As soon as we appoint a marshal, he has jurisdiction inside the townsite. Collie has it outside. The city council will pass a new ordinance for you saying it's against the law for a saloon to shelter prostitutes. I think that's what whores are called in court. All you do is enforce that ordinance. Let him build a saloon, but you keep the whores out. He'll be busted in six months if he hasn't got the girls. If it gets to rough stuff, my boys will give you all the help you want. How does that sound?"

While Maule was talking, Pete was listening, but he was also thinking. If he took the job he would be so close to Maule it would be like living in his pocket. He would never have a chance to be closer. He could ask for privacy with Maule and get it. He would, in effect, be Maule's closest bodyguard.

Pete shrugged now and said, "It sounds good enough. I always said I'd try anything once and I've never tried being a marshal."

Maule laughed. He reached in the right-hand drawer of his desk, took out something and tossed it on the desk top.

One look at it told Pete he had just been given his badge of office.

"Who swears me in?"

Maule smiled. "Why, Bill French. He's acting mayor. Didn't you hear him swear you in?" He leaned over, picked up the badge and tossed it to Pete, who caught it. "Walk out of here wearing it, Pete. The sooner everybody knows it the better."

Pete pinned on the badge and momentarily felt a fool. The office of marshal, however minor, carried certain responsibilities that should be acknowledged by solemn oath and witnessed. Instead, here was this travesty.

"By the way, Pete," Maule said idly. "The council drew up a new ordinance while you were seeing Collie. I want you to enforce it."

"What does it say?"

Maule smiled. "It's being printed up already. You'll get a copy this afternoon."

Pete only nodded and asked, "Where do I work out of?"

"Otey Collins is clearing out a back storeroom that opens onto the alley. It's just a few feet from the street. He'll have a sign hung on the corner of the building where everybody can see it from the street. By this afternoon he'll have you a desk and some chairs. By tomorrow, warrant forms will be printed up. This afternoon I'll take a map over to the surveyor and have him ink in the townsite boundaries."

"What do I use for a jail if I need one?"

"Why, the county's. We're in the county and any arrest you make will be made in the county too. What have I missed?"

Pete shook his head. "I'm the last man to know that."

Maule stood up. "Show yourself around town, Pete. When anybody asks about the badge, tell them the council called you in. You didn't apply for the job, you were offered it and took it."

Maule extended his hand and said with a smile, "Congratulations, Marshal."

They shook hands. Pete, in spite of himself, felt a touch of loathing for himself that all conspirators feel. He turned and was halfway to the door when Maule said, "One more thing, Pete. Just remember that badge doesn't make you bullet-proof."

"Your old housemen, you mean?"

"I reckon I do," Maule said.

Out in the corridor Pete halted by the bodyguard who had taken his gun. The guard had it halfway extended when he caught sight of the badge. "What's that?" he asked slowly.

Pete reached for his gun and said, "Get somebody to read it for you." Then Pete looked at the other three guards and said, "That's the last time you'll lift my gun, any of you."

They looked at his badge and then at each other and Pete walked out into the blazing heat of noon.

He was already late for dinner, he knew, and he dreaded this necessity of a late entrance into the boarding house dining room. It would seem to all the boarders and to Laurie and Aunt Martha that he had staged his lateness so he could impress all of them with this new shiny badge. He thought first of eating elsewhere and letting the news of his appointment get around during the afternoon. Or he could take off the badge just this once. And then he knew that he must face them sooner or later and get it over with.

He took the walkway, entered the house, hung his hat on

the wall among the other hats and went into the dining room. As he halted, looking for an empty chair, the room fell silent until Moynihan spoke up.

"I can't read it from here, Pete. What does it say?"

"Marshal," Pete said and moved toward the empty chair next to Moynihan. He was sitting down as Laurie came in with the coffeepot. She smiled at him, saw the badge, and stopped abruptly.

Moynihan said wryly, "We got a brand-new lawman with us, Laurie."

Laurie stood motionless, her attention on the badge, then lifted her glance to Pete's face. "Where—where did you get that, Pete?"

"From the town council," Pete said. Then he turned his head to Moynihan and said, "Please pass the meat, Moynihan."

"Yes, *sir,*" Moynihan said, mockery in his voice.

When Moynihan passed the platter of steaks to him and while Pete was helping himself, Moynihan said, "So you're why the boss asked me to set up warrant forms just before dinner."

"I suppose so," Pete said idly. He was watching Laurie now as she poured the coffee. When she finished filling each boarder's cup, she would glance at him and, seeing Pete watching her, her glance would slide away. The talk in the dining room began again and some of the boarders, finished with their meal, began to move out of the room.

Moynihan declined a second cup of coffee, but waited until Laurie had filled Pete's cup and moved on. When she was out of earshot, Moynihan said, "I'm glad I took the trouble to recommend Maule to you last night. I'm glad you took my advice."

His tone was one of withering sarcasm and Pete felt a sudden anger, then checked it. He would have to get used to this because there was more coming. He said mildly, "It's a job and that's something I don't have."

"And killing Burns was just a warm-up for the job?"

"Why, of course," Pete said dryly. "Why else would I have killed him?"

Moynihan said, "Agh," in disgust, rose and walked out of the room.

Again, because he was so late, Pete was left to finish his meal alone save for Laurie who was clearing dishes on both tables. When she came to removing Moynihan's plate, she didn't speak nor did Pete. When all the dishes were cleared except Pete's, she came back with the coffeepot and asked, "More coffee?"

"No thanks, but sit down, Laurie."

As Pete moved his plate and cup away from him, Laurie sat down and put down the coffeepot. Without looking at her, Pete said, "Say it, Laurie."

"They say you killed a man in the street in a gun fight."

Pete looked full at Laurie now. She was paler than usual and the whites of her dark eyes were faintly red as if she had been crying.

"Did they tell you who he was?"

"A man named Burns. What did you have against him that you'd shoot him?"

Quietly Pete told her who Burns was and why the fired houseman had picked the fight.

Laurie listened soberly and when he was finished, said, "But did you have to kill him?"

Patiently, Pete explained that because Burns had a split-second advantage of the draw, he himself hadn't time to aim, and that his snap shot had the misfortune to kill Burns instead of wounding him.

Laurie accepted this with the same soberness she had accepted the circumstances of the fight. Now she asked, "Did the town council make you marshal before or after you shot Burns?"

"After."

"Then that explains it," Laurie said. "They hired you because you were good and fast with a pistol, didn't they?"

Pete knew that if he told Laurie the truth, that he was

Maule's stopper for Collier's ambitions, he would put himself in a worse light than he was in now.

"Maybe, but one shot doesn't make a gun fighter, Laurie."

"Did Maule get you the job?"

Ever since that first night when Laurie had hidden Pete in her room, he had sworn to himself he would not lie to her unless the answers to her questions jeopardized his mission. What he was about to say would be a half lie because, indirectly, it did involve his job here. He said then, "I expect he did, Laurie. I told you he promised he'd find something for me. This is that something."

Anger mounted swiftly in Laurie's eyes. "What a something!" she said in disgust. "What favor does he expect from you in return?"

Now he would have to lie, Pete knew. "I don't know."

"You do know," Laurie said flatly. "Why haven't we had a marshal for the last five years? Why does Maule recommend you to his council when he's only known you for three days? What are you hiding, Pete? Come to that, who are you?"

"Just what you see."

"You know what I see," Laurie countered. "I see an intelligent man who's attracted by corruption and is willing to be corrupted himself."

From what she'd seen of him, that was a fair assessment, Pete thought. In the light of all his secret dealings with Maule, it was even a charitable one.

"I told you once, Laurie, when Maule gave me the first job, that nobody's going to make me do what I don't want to do. That still holds. How do you know I won't make a good marshal?"

"Because the men who appointed you are all Ben Maule's men, body and soul. They wouldn't have appointed you unless you were Maule's man too."

"Wait and see if I am, Laurie."

"Why, you are now or you wouldn't be wearing that badge."

"You want me to leave this house, Laurie?"

Laurie looked startled, then recovered herself. "Do you want to leave?"

"No, I like it here. I like the people staying here and I like my room. I like the food but, especially, I like you."

They looked at each other a long moment and Pete was suddenly aware that what he had said had brought a blush to Laurie's face and neck. She rose now and said in a matter-of-fact tone of voice, "You need a place to eat and sleep and Aunt Martha and I need the money. Move if you like but not because you think we want you out. I—I even promise to stay out of your affairs."

Pete looked up at her and smiled. "If you do, I'll move."

Laurie smiled shyly, reached over, picked up his plate and cup and took them into the kitchen. When she didn't return, Pete left for his room. He would stay here for the present, he thought, but something in the future, some order from Ben Maule, would make it necessary for him to leave, and that was a pity, for of all the people he had met here, only Laurie was not flawed.

Once in his room, Pete sat down on the bed and began to strip the bandages from his hands. His thoughts, however, still lingered on his conversation with Laurie. What had made him tell her that of all things here, he liked her best? Was it the cheapest kind of flattery, a kind of insurance against being asked to leave? He didn't think so, for without her affectionate friendship, these past few days would have been a lengthy and dangerous cypher. He could not imagine what it would be like to lose her friendship, although he knew that what he would be forced to do in the future would inevitably part them.

Beyond that, weren't his feelings for Laurie a disloyalty to the memory of Anne? Five days ago he would have staked everything he owned or ever would own that after Anne's death no other woman would hold any interest for him. In other men who had lost a wife, he had seen time slowly erode the memory of the loss and he had always felt a contempt for their allowing this to happen. Was the same thing beginning to happen to him? Was this nature's way of making life livable for the grieving? He couldn't be sure of that, but of one thing he was certain; Laurie Mays cared about what he did and what was happening to him.

He looked at his hands now and saw that most of the swelling was gone and the skin healed over and closed. He could do without the bandages and was glad for that. They had marked him as a brawler. He didn't doubt that Burns, this morning, had counted on his hurt, bandaged hands to slow down his draw. From now on, though, nobody could claim he was hiding behind his bandages.

8

Pete waited until midafternoon to visit his new office in Otey Collins' store. Instead of going through the store, which was on the Main Street corner of the same side street block as the hotel, he took the side street and entered the alley. Maule had been right in saying that the alley entrance to the office was only a few feet from the back corner of the building. The door was unlocked and Pete stepped inside.

A much used roll-top desk, lamp atop it, had been placed between the two barred windows that looked out on the side street. He supposed the bars had been placed there to prevent break-ins and looting, but they were grimly appropriate. A leather-covered sofa, leaking stuffing, was against the alley wall, a straight-backed chair facing the room was to the immediate left of the desk, while a comfortable armchair was on the desk's right. The floor, surprisingly, was con-

structed of big squares of Mexican red title. The desk chair
was a swivel one with arms. A calendar on the whitewashed
wall and a brass cuspidor by the desk completed the furnishings. Everything looked faintly shabby and used.

Pete hung his hat on the wall nail, moved to the desk and
was checking the drawers when there came a knock on the
door that led into the store. Even before he could speak, the
door opened and a middle-aged man, a box under one arm,
crossed over to the desk.

As he passed Pete, he said, "I'm Ames Williams, Marshal. Let me dump this stuff." He deposited the box filled
with legal forms and block-lettered signs on the desk top,
then turned and extended his hand. Pete shook hands with
him and tried to remember what Moynihan had said of his
boss. He was, of course, Maule's man, perhaps thirty-five
and of a blocky build, bushy-haired and blue-eyed.

"Have a chair," Pete said and added, "You're my first
caller."

"Then I hope I bring you luck," Williams said. He sat
down in the armchair and surveyed this almost bare room.
Then he looked at Pete with a frank curiosity in his eyes.
"Ben says I ought to do a piece on you for the *Banner,*
especially after that shooting this morning." He paused.
"He says you've been to prison. That won't get in the *Banner,* of course, but is it true?"

"What difference would it make if it is?" Pete asked.

Williams shrugged with apparent indifference, reached in
his shirt pocket for a pencil and picked up one of the legal
forms he had just delivered, folded it for a note pad and
said, "You ever been a lawman?"

Pete only shook his head in negation, moved over to the
swivel chair and sat down.

"Well, what's your background?"

"Nobody cares what it is," Pete said. "Why do you?"

"Well, I've got to write something about you, man."

"My history starts four days back. Moynihan can tell you
all about me."

"He already has. You crippled one of the Crossfire housemen, then got his job. You took on a couple of miners in a saloon brawl and because the housemen wouldn't help you, Ben fired them. One of them tried to gun you down today and lost."

"That's the way it happened," Pete agreed.

"But before that?"

Pete shook his head. "Nothing that's worth writing about." Pete knew that as long as he was in Ben Maule's good graces he didn't have to worry about what Ames Williams would write of him in the *Banner*. Maule might want to make a kind of hero out of him in order to reflect credit on his tame council, but Pete doubted it.

"Maybe I'm a better judge of that than you are," Williams said with a smile. "Why don't you just talk about yourself?"

"No, I've seen this happen before," Pete said. "A new lawman with a tough reputation is hired to ride herd on the town. Then's when he starts to draw flies, you might say."

Williams grinned. "If I understand, you mean all the young studs with a gun try to take him on."

"Exactly."

"But you've already taken on Larry Burns and won. Where did you learn how to do it?"

"Let's leave it right there," Pete said. "I wasn't a marshal then, so it was just a street fight."

"You want me to keep that fight out of the paper?"

"No, it's around already."

"Well, what qualifications do you have for the job?"

"None."

"But you were hired because you killed him, because you're a gun fighter, weren't you?" Williams insisted.

"Nobody mentioned that to me."

"Then why did you take the job?"

"So I can eat," Pete said calmly.

"But man, I can't—" Williams stopped talking and stared past him toward the door into the store. Pete turned then and saw what had attracted Williams' gaze. Lace Ferrill was standing in the store entrance doorway. She was wearing a gray lace-collared dress the same color as the tiny hat perched on top of her red hair and was carrying a folded parasol.

Williams said familiarly, "Hi, Lace." Pete gave a reserved, "Afternoon." Williams looked at Pete and said, "Thanks for nothing, but take care of yourself."

He rose, went out past Lace. Pete said, "Come to see my new office?"

She only nodded; then, moving into the room, she said, "I overheard a lot of that."

"Didn't tell you much, did it?"

Lace smiled and then, to Pete's surprise, she reached out and closed the door that led into the store. Without being invited, she moved past Pete and sat down in the armchair the editor had just vacated. "You can't blame Ames for being curious about you, Pete. The whole town is."

"Well, I'm curious about you, but I've never asked you to tell me about yourself."

Lace seemed to ignore this as she had her brief look at the bare furnishings of the room. "You should ask Josh to give you some of the beer and whisky posters they're always sending him. For your bare walls."

Pete moved over to the swivel chair and slacked into it. "But I'm not running a saloon."

"They'd brighten up the room, though."

"And send my callers over to the Crossfire?"

Lace smiled. "I hadn't thought of that, but I guess it would."

"Well, now that you've decorated my office for me, what can I do for you?"

Lace studied him for several moments in silence before she said, "I have the feeling you came to Banning because Ben Maule is here."

The surprise that came into Pete's face was genuine, but not for the reasons Lace would assume. He felt the cold touch of alarm as her words registered. Had his moves been that transparent? If Maule felt the same way as Lace did, he was in for big trouble. With an effort to keep his tone and voice normal, he said in a tone of puzzlement, "Tell me why you think that?"

"Well, you took dead aim on Ben the first day you were here. I've watched you tie yourself closer to Ben with everything you've done."

"Why wouldn't I?" Pete asked bluntly. "When I got here, close to broke, I asked the question anybody that's half-bright would ask—who runs the town?"

"And they told you Ben?"

"Everyone. Long ago when I was saddle tramping around between big outfits, I learned one thing—never hit the foreman for a job. Always hit up the owner. In this case, Ben Maule was the owner and I went to him." He paused and added quietly, "I've got a feeling you did the same thing."

A glint of anger came into Lace's eyes and was gone. She laughed softly. "That hurt a little, but it's true," she said. She leaned forward in the chair, resting her elbows on her knees. "Well, why did you come to Banning at all?"

"I'll turn that right back at you," Pete said. "Why did you choose Banning?"

"Why, there's big money to be made in mining camps."

"And there're a lot of mining camps. Why this one?"

"You answer that first," Lace said coolly.

"Fair enough. A while back I made a big mistake and had to jump the country where I made it. I'd heard of this camp and I knew it was close to the border. If they catch up with me I can drift over there, but until they do, I'd rather earn dollars than pesos."

"What sort of a mistake?"

Pete shook his head. "No."

"All right then, that's pretty much my story too."

Pete smiled faintly. "Let's see which one of us can hang on the longest."

Lace rose. There was one more question Pete wanted to

ask her, but it was too risky. The question was, had Ben Maule sent her? Maybe he could put it indirectly. As he walked with her to the door, he said, "Tell Ben why I'm here."

She turned her head to look at him, a faint surprise in her face. "I won't tell him anything. I'm supposed to be shopping." Then she hesitated. "Yes, I will. I'll tell him I poked my head in here to look at your new office. Williams was here with you, I'll tell him."

The question was answered. Ben hadn't sent her and Pete felt a vast relief. He said easily, "Well, I'd like to see your place sometime, too."

She said coldly, "Better not."

"Ben?"

She looked at him long and seriously, and finally seemed to come to her decision. She reached up, buried her hand in the lace collar of her dress, then unbuttoned the second button of her dress. What Pete saw made him wince, for her throat and the area below it were hideously disfigured by scars left by knife cuts.

"Ben gave me these for entertaining a man at my house. He said if he caught me entertaining another man, he'd move up to my face."

Pete's glance lifted from the cuts to her still face. "What happened to the man you entertained?"

"Ben had him killed," Lace said quietly. She buttoned up her dress, fastened the collar and the scars were hidden again.

Pete risked a question then. "After that, do you even like him?"

"Don't I have to?" Lace said, almost with indifference.

"I guess you do," Pete agreed. He opened the door for her, she nodded her goodbye and stepped into the store proper.

Pete went back to his chair and sat down, trying to make sense out of what he had just seen and heard. In the first place, why had she come to see him without Maule's knowledge? Was it her woman's pride that made her believe she could learn things about him that the sometimes obtuse Maule wouldn't think of ferreting out? Was she trying to protect Maule by attempting to test his loyalty to Maule? Or was she searching for any indication that he was here on account of Maule's presence so that she could join him against Maule?

Certainly the revelation of the knife scars on her throat had been not only startling but unnecessary. Too, her answer to his question if she even liked Maule after this disfigurement of her was a strange one. Was she trying to tell him something without really saying it?

Maybe, just maybe, she was the key to the isolation and capture of Maule. But if he made a mistake with her, she could be the key to his own death.

He turned his attention to the stuff Williams had left on his desk. Under the warrant forms was a folded map. He spread it out on the desk and saw that it was a map of Banning and that surrounding areas and mines and claims were recorded. But what was more important, the town boundaries had been drawn in red ink. Whoever had staked the townsite, he saw, had anticipated nothing short of the growth of a city, for it was a big townsite.

Folding the map and making a mental note to tack it above his desk, Pete picked up the last piece of paper. It was a proof sheet and contained very little print. Boldface type proclaimed Ordinance Number 23. It stated:

BY ORDER OF THE TOWN COUNCIL
ALL FEMALES EMPLOYED IN AN
ESTABLISHMENT THAT DISPENSES
SPIRITS WITHIN THE TOWN LIMITS
OF BANNING MUST HAVE A WORKING
PERMIT ISSUED BY THE TOWN
COUNCIL

Pete laughed out loud. The ordinance was, of course, aimed at Collier and his plan. It would be simple enough for

Maule's council to issue permits to Lace and the Mexican waitresses at the Bonanza Hotel. Even the girls in the North End cribs would remain untouched. But let Collier open a new saloon with girls inside the town limits, no permits would be issued them. If the sheriff wanted a new saloon with girls, he would have to build it more than a mile from the center of town, and in spite of the hundreds of horses and mules here, they were mostly company-owned and unavailable to the mass of miners. A two-mile walk at the end of a laboring day would hardly be an attraction to the average miner, even if there were girls involved. Maule, Pete reflected, had neatly revenged himself on Collier for his disloyalty. Maule was not only a hard man but a clever one.

Almost the last item in the box was a pair of handcuffs with a key. Picking them up, Pete wondered where Maule had got them. Then he remembered there had been a town marshal here many years ago and he supposed they had belonged to him.

He pulled open a drawer and was about to pitch them in it when he realized how foolish this would be. If the handcuffs were to be of any use, they had to be on the arresting officer's person. If he needed them, he wouldn't have time to run back here to get them. Reluctantly he rose and rammed them in his hip pocket along with the key. The remaining item in the box was a pair of keys tied together with a buckskin thong. They would be for the two doors of his office, he assumed.

He was putting away the papers in a drawer when the alley door opened abruptly. Glancing over his shoulder, Pete saw Sheriff Collier standing in the doorway. Collier gave the room the briefest look and then tramped over to Pete's desk. He had a paper in his hand which he slapped down on the desk top, saying, "Williams just left this."

Pete glanced at it and saw that it was a copy of the ordinance and looked up at the sheriff. "He left me one too."

The sheriff said in a quiet but anger-choked voice, "You're wearing Maule's badge, so you were in on this too."

"That's right. Sit down and I'll answer any questions you ask."

Collier took the armchair and, facing Pete, studied him for a wrathful moment. "That was Ben's money you showed me this morning, wasn't it?"

Pete nodded. "I'm surprised you didn't guess it."

"You were only spying for him?"

"Absolutely."

The sheriff scowled and said slowly, "Just who the hell are you?"

"A man just as hungry as you are. Maybe even hungrier."

"You think you'll get any help from me in this new job?"

"I don't remember asking for it."

"You'll have to. You'll need my jail."

"I'll get it too," Pete said. "Banning is in your county so any crime committed in the town is committed in the county."

"Oh, no," the sheriff said flatly. "You pick up a fighting drunk at the Crossfire, then he's in your town. There's nothing in my book that says I have to pick him up."

"I'll make you a present of him," Pete said pleasantly.

"Try it," the sheriff dared.

"I will," Pete said. "If you give me any trouble, then I'm going to close up the North End cribs."

Sheriff Collier came to his feet. "We'll see how much muscle you've got, sonny."

"I think you will," Pete said mildly.

Sheriff Collier stalked to the door, opened it, and slammed it viciously behind him.

9

Since the noon meal when word was brought of Pete's killing of Burns, Aunt Martha had gone about her chores in grim silence, Laurie observed. When the kitchen was cleaned up, Aunt Martha had climbed up to her room for her afternoon nap. Once her own chores were done, Laurie went to her room too and lay down on the bed to rest.

She thought she knew what was going on in her aunt's mind. She and her aunt were rightly proud and jealous of the reputation of their place. Not only were the roomers carefully chosen, but the boarders were too. All of a sudden they had a man in their midst who had killed a man in a gun fight. As Pete had explained to her, he was only defending himself, but the fact remained he had killed a man. It wasn't true that Pete was one of the brawling gun-fighting scum that Aunt Martha hated, but all his actions since he had been living here seemed to prove he was. Added to that, he was Maule's marshal, which would be another big black mark against him in Aunt Martha's book.

Laurie, with a sad wisdom, knew that as marshal, Pete would get into still more trouble and when he did, Aunt Martha's patience would run out. She would ask him to leave. If he left, something strange and wonderful would go out of Laurie's life, and she dreaded the thought. She knew in her heart that he wasn't a bad man; on the contrary, he was gentle and good. Well, she decided, there was nothing she could do to alter circumstances in the future. All she could do was wait.

Not wanting to sleep, she slept, and wakened only when it was time for her to help prepare for the evening meal. As usual, Pete came in late. Could it be, Laurie wondered, that he was making a practice of this so he could talk with her after the others had cleared out? As she went about waiting at the tables, she hoped this was true, for it meant he wanted her company.

Laurie cleaned up the dishes of the last diner as Pete was drinking his coffee. Returning from the kitchen, she poured him a second cup and then, as at this noon, sat down to join him. She was wondering as she sank into the chair if her flare of temper this noon had altered his friendly feeling toward her, but when she saw his smile of welcome, she guessed it had not.

"Laurie, I got to thinking about you today. Do you ever get out of this house?"

"Why, of course. Aunt Martha and I shop every third day."

"Besides that, though?"

"Sundays, I go to church in the Masonic Hall."

"Besides that, though," Pete persisted.

"Why, no," Laurie said. "What's there to do?"

"Have you ever had a good look at this town?"

"All that I want to see."

"Tell you what. While you help Aunt Martha clean up, I'll go down to the livery and rent a rig, and we'll drive around until dark. If I'm going to be marshal of this place, I have to learn something about it. When it gets dark I'll show you my new office. How does that sound?"

A smile of pleasure came into Laurie's face and she said, "That would be fun, Pete. Let's do it."

Pete, leaving his second cup of coffee untouched, rose and said, "We can use all the daylight left. I'll hurry."

In the kitchen Laurie came up to her aunt who was drying dishes at the sink and said, "Aunt Martha, I'm going for a drive with Pete. He has to learn the town and I'm going to show it to him."

Her Aunt Martha had her lips parted ready to say something when Laurie raised a hand. "I know what you're going to say, but if the town marshal can't protect me, who can?"

"You don't know what I was going to say," Aunt Martha said. "I was going to say it was about time you got away from this kitchen. Go ahead."

Laurie went into the bedroom and changed from her drab gray work dress into a blue print dress spangled with tiny cornflowers. She was waiting in one of the veranda chairs when Pete drove up in a buggy with its top up. He stepped down, still holding the reins, and handed her up, then climbed in beside her. "You're the guide," he said.

"Let's go the way we're headed, but not on Main Street."

They kept on the same street and a block past the boarding house was a high wall under towering cottonwoods fed by the *Acquia's* water. Through wrought-iron gates they could see a blooming garden in the patio of an L-shaped one-story house with *portal.*

Laurie looked at him and said dryly, "If you ever need to find Ben Maule at night, there's where to look first."

"Who lives there?"

"Why, who else but Lace Ferrill?"

"I thought he had a ranch south of town."

"He's got a woman *in* town," Laurie said tartly.

They kept to other side streets and Pete was soon to learn that Laurie knew a good bit about the sprawling town. She explained how the immigrant groups tended to seek out their countrymen and, like animals, stake out part of the town as their own. She pointed out to Pete that he would see few children playing, for unless these miners married Mexican women, they were wifeless and womanless. A very few had been able to send back to the old country for their women.

The rutted streets or, rather, tracks they drove through took them past a jumble of tents, tent dormitories and an adobe dormitory, in front of which a dozen men were pitching horseshoes, a big barren cemetery, and a fenced collection pond for the waters pumped from the mines. By the time they had circled the town, the big coal-oil flares that lighted the mine buildings up on the slopes of the Padres were lighted. As they reached the heart of the town, avoiding the main road and its dust, it was dark. Pete picked his way along the side streets and pulled up his rig in the alley where the new marshal's office was located. It had been a pleasant drive, Laurie thought, but she had talked too much. Of course, her chatter was in answer to Pete's questions, but still she talked like a teacher, with Pete her only pupil.

Pete handed her down, tied the horse to the loading dock and moved in the darkness toward the door. He struck a match to find the keyhole and by its light, Laurie saw a big cardboard sign nailed to the door: TOWN MARSHAL'S OFFICE it proclaimed in big block letters on heavy cardboard.

The door unlocked, Pete pocketed the key, and while the match was still burning, extended his hand to Laurie. She took it, feeling its roughness and warmth, and then the flame died. Pete led her inside, halted and struck another match and lighted the lamp atop the desk. As he raised the lamp wick to give more light, Laurie looked around the sparsely furnished room. She had been in it once before when it was jammed with barrels from floor to ceiling. "Why, it's really a nice room, Pete. Where did they put all the stuff that was in here?"

"I haven't asked," Pete said. "Nobody's tried the sofa, Laurie. See if it falls down with you."

"You've already had callers, then?" Laurie said, walking toward the sofa. She sat down, and when Pete didn't answer immediately, she looked at him.

"Two men and a woman," he said cryptically and moved over to the swivel chair, put his hat on the desk top and turned the chair toward her.

"A woman? Who was it?"

Pete was silent a long moment as if he were hesitant to tell her, Laurie thought. Finally he said, "Lace Ferrill stopped by to look at my new office."

"Why would she, for heaven's sake?"

"A woman's curiosity, I'd guess."

"Well, I've got some too," Laurie said. "What did you talk about?"

Pete gave her a somber look and said, "Nothing much."

"But what?" Laurie insisted.

"She wanted me to decorate my walls with some of Josh Eddy's whisky and beer posters."

"But you aren't running a saloon."

"That's what I told her." Pete stood up, picked up his hat and said, "Well, that's all there is to see, Laurie. I'd better get you home."

Laurie had the feeling that Pete was reluctant to talk about Lace Ferrill and she wondered why. There was more to her visit than talk of decorating his office, Laurie guessed. She rose and Pete reached for the lamp and lifted it off the desk.

"I'll light you out," he said as he crossed over in front of her, opened the door, stepped out into the night and stood there holding the lamp while she came out into the alley.

Side by side they moved toward the buggy. Then Pete halted and caught her arm. His rough abruptness startled Laurie and she looked at him. "No buggy," Pete said quietly. "Turn around and go back in the office. Hurry!" Frightened by the urgency in Pete's voice, Laurie obeyed, and had not taken two steps toward the door when he vanished with the lamp.

Pete moved over to the loading dock, set the lamp on it, then knelt in the shelter of the dock's timbers and drew his gun. Closing his eyes now in an effort to wipe out the lamp's glare, he listened and reflected. From the far end of the loading dock came the faint sound of a horse moving in its harness, and Pete reckoned the rig was tied over there. Who had moved it?

The reason it had been moved was fairly obvious. Whoever was waiting out there had counted on Pete, lamp in hand, searching for the missing rig. He would have made a self-lighted target. Somewhere then, around the end of the loading dock, his man would be waiting.

He opened his eyes now and looked to his left toward the side street. There was enough light cast by the lamps of the hotel for him to be silhouetted if he attempted to cross the alley. The same held true if he walked down the alley toward his rig. Would it hold true if he climbed onto the loading dock, and hugging the wall, moved down the dock? Probably, but it was a chance he would have to take.

Moving back against the wall now, he hoisted himself onto the loading dock and flattened himself against the adobe wall. Moving sideways, he took cautious steps toward the far end of the sixty-foot loading dock.

In the bay made by one of the big padlocked doors, his shoulder touched something that was not a part of the door and he shifted his gun to his left hand and pawed out with his right. Immediately he touched the handle of a broom. Hefting it, he could tell by its weight that it was one of those heavy wide push brooms.

He shifted his gun back to his right hand and, lifting the broom in his left, continued his slow way. The nightly racket from the Crossfire a half-block away was, while muffled, still enough sound to cover the occasional scuffing of his boots on the uneven planking. By now, his eyes were adjusted to the night and he could make out the rig some twenty feet ahead of him.

And then he came to the second bay made by the big storeroom doors. This, he reckoned, was where he must make his move. Whoever was waiting for him was likely forted up across the way in the deep shadow of the hotel's outbuildings abutting the alley.

Ramming his gun in his belt, Pete lifted the broom, his right hand against the butt of the handle, and sailed it arcing at the livery horse. He could not see it land but he heard it. The horse gave a snort of surprise and there was a quick drumming of its hoofs as it skittered sideways, exploding at the same time with a frightened neigh.

Abruptly, a dim figure raised up from its hiding place at the far end of the loading platform and ran toward the now rearing horse.

Pete lifted his gun and, with no sighting possible, pointed it at the man and pulled the trigger. He heard the great grunting cough of the figure as it pitched forward into the alley.

Only seconds after his shot, a gun roar erupted from across the alley and Pete heard the slug slam into the timber storeroom door by his elbow. Immediately Pete fell to his knees and then flattened out on his belly, facing the alley. A second, third, and fourth shot came from across the alley, the slugs searching him out as they slammed into the doors. The orange gun flare of each shot came from the same spot. When the fifth shot came, Pete had his pistol aimed at the spot and he fired in instant retaliation.

He heard a muffled cry and then a crash, as if a weight had fallen on stacked lumber and toppled it. Instantly Pete was on his feet, his legs driving. Leaping off the loading dock, he headed for the dark block of the building across the alley, aiming to the right of the place where the gunfire had come from. When he reached the building, he turned and moved carefully to its corner, his gun held ahead of him, and again he heard the clatter of boards. He reached into his jacket pocket for a match, remembering that his ambusher had shot five of his six loads.

Pete lifted his knee, which drew his trousers taut against his thigh. On the cloth of it he wiped the match alight and, holding it up, moved his head around the corner. By its sputtering flare, he saw a man lying on the scattered boards he had toppled. He had fallen on his back, feet to the alley, and had raised himself on his elbows. The gun was in his hand and Pete saw it point toward the match. He pulled back just as the shot came, clipping the corner of the building and scattering pulverized adobe in his face.

Immediately Pete lunged around the corner, and remembering the man's position, made a spread-eagled smothering dive at the spot. He landed heavily on the man's body and heard at the same time an anguished cry of pain. With his right forearm against the man's throat, he searched with his left for the pistol which, its barrel still hot, was burning his belly. Wrenching it free, he threw it back of him into the alley and then came to his knees astride the man.

Again he reached in his jacket pocket for a match, leaned down and struck it alight on one of the boards beneath him. Pete was looking into the white, strained and frightened face of Bill Shields, one of the fired Crossfire housemen. The match still burning in his hand, Pete came off Shields and rose. "Get up."

"I can't. I'm hit in the leg."

Pete saw the blood-soaked right pants leg. "I can see that. I think you can walk. Get up." As the match died, Pete shifted his gun to his left hand, bunched up the collar of Shield's jacket, and hauled him roughly to his feet. Shields groaned with pain, but when Pete let go of him, Shields was able to sustain his own weight.

Moving behind him, Pete put his gun in the middle of Shields's back and said, "Now walk." Shields, a tall, raw-boned man, tried to take a step and fell on his knees, crying out in pain.

Pete said coldly, "Pick up a board. Use it for a crutch." Again he struck a match and, by its light, Shields found a weathered board before the match went out. Hauling him to his feet now, Pete let him fit the board under his arm and then prodded him into motion, saying, "Head for the rig."

Laboriously, Shields moved ahead, limping out into the alley. Pete, keeping behind him, said, "Sing out to your partner. Tell him if he shoots, I shoot you."

"Don't shoot, Frank!" Shields called. "If you do, he'll shoot me."

Shields got in motion again and again Pete stayed behind him, using him as a shield. They made their slow way up to the buggy. Behind him, Pete could hear people coming down the alley. Now that the shooting had ceased they were doubtless coming to see what had happened.

Pete prodded Shields around the livery horse and then saw the man lying face down in the alley dust alongside the horse. Striking his match against the buggy's dashboard, Pete moved over to the downed man. A great wet circle of blood stained the back of his shirt and Pete moved over and turned the heavy body on its back. He didn't have to check the pulse to know that Frank Becker, next to the last of the housemen, was dead.

The match died and Pete said to Shields, "Climb in that buggy." To the first of the half-dozen men who now came around the buggy to have their look, he said, "Give me a hand here, will you. Let's put him on the loading platform."

Ramming his gun in his belt, he took Becker's legs while two men took his arms. They hoisted his bulky body onto the platform and afterward Pete moved over to the buggy. Shields had a foot on the back step, but could not lift himself, and Pete gave him a boost onto the buggy seat.

From out of the gathering crowd, a voice rose above the chatter. "Where are you taking him, Marshal?"

Pete recognized it as the voice of Sheriff Collier, and he said, "To jail."

"Not my jail," Collier said flatly.

"I think so," Pete said.

In the darkness Pete could distinguish no faces, but his interest centered on the short slight figure of a boy. Moving over to him, Pete said, "Want to earn a dollar, son?"

"Sure."

"Run over to Doc Price's office. Go around in back where he lives. Tell him to come over to the jail."

Someone in the crowd said sarcastically, "That's a pretty good score for the day, Marshal. Would you call it two and a half?"

Pete ignored him, moving over to untie the rig. As he climbed into the buggy and took the reins, he called, "Watch it, I'm turning around."

The crowd moved to let the buggy make its half circle. As it finished, Pete suddenly remembered Laurie. When he came abreast of his office door, he reined in and saw Laurie's dim figure framing the open doorway of the dark room. "Wait for me, Laurie," he called. "I won't be long."

There was no answer and he got the rig in motion. Leaving the alley, he crossed the street and drew up in front of the sheriff's office. Sheriff Collier, who had followed the buggy, ducked under the tie rail heading for his lamplit office.

"Don't lock the door on me, Sheriff. I'll shoot the lock off."

Collier acted as if he hadn't heard. Pete helped Shields down, followed him through a break in the tie rail, then skirted him and opened the door to the sheriff's office. Pete let Shields limp in before him and then entered himself.

Collier had swung his chair away from the desk to face the room.

"Take him out of here. I won't lock him up."

Pete moved past Shields, whose head was hung in weariness and despair. The door to the cell block was open and Pete said, "Come on, Shields."

While Shields limped toward him, Pete moved over to the closest of the three cells. Testing the barred cell door, he found it unlocked and swung it open. He waited in the doorway while Shields limped inside. Collier had halted in the doorway, watching as Shields moved over to the cot and settled on it with a shuddering grunt.

"I told you, you get no keys. He's not my prisoner," Collier said roughly.

"I heard you," Pete said. He walked into the cell and said to Shields, "Lie down."

"If you'll swing my leg up," Shields said in a shaky voice.

Pete lifted his leg onto the cot and with a grimace of pain, Shields stretched out. Then Pete shoved the cot into the back corner.

"Put your hands over your head," Pete said to Shields.

Shields did and his hands touched the bars which separated this cell from the next one.

From his hip pocket Pete drew out the handcuffs, rummaged around for the key, found it and opened the cuffs. Around Shields's left wrist he put one of the handcuffs and the other, connected to it by a short chain, he put around the cell bars, then locked both cuffs. Shields was as securely in jail as if the cell door had been locked.

Pete now glanced up and saw a look of wrath on Collier's face as he stood in the corridor, watching this. Pete stepped out into the corridor and said, "Doc Price is coming. I'll leave a dollar on your desk for the boy that brings him." He turned, put the money on the sheriff's desk, and left the building.

As Pete climbed into the rig and picked up the reins, he sat motionless for several seconds. He was about to face Laurie and what could he say to her? He remembered what the man in the alley had called to him: "That makes two and a half for today, don't it, Marshal?" The man was right, and yet what could he have done to prevent any of this happening?

In the alley he tied the horse to the loading dock. Beyond, the very door that had taken Shields's slugs was open, and by the lighted lantern inside, Pete saw the men carrying the body of Becker inside to the hardware store which served as the town's undertaking parlor.

He found the lamp where he had left it on the dock, lighted it and moved into his office. Laurie had been sitting in the darkness in the armchair beside the desk. Her face was pale and strained, and along with the hurt in her eyes was something else that Pete could not quite read—a mixture of contempt, fear, and disbelief. He said, "I'm sorry you had to be here when this happened, Laurie. It was not my making."

"Were—were they after you?"

Pete nodded. "Two more of the Crossfire housemen."

"They say you killed one man and hurt another."

Again Pete nodded and then said bitterly, "A man in the crowd out there named my score as two and a half in one day."

"That's what I was thinking," Laurie said quietly.

"I'm not proud of it, Laurie, but they want me dead."

"You could always quit and leave here."

"I can't, Laurie. Don't ask me why, I just can't." He paused. "You'd like to go home now, wouldn't you?"

She only nodded and rose and now, as before, Pete preceded her out with the lamp and then handed her into the buggy. He returned the lamp to the office, blew out its flame, locked the door and climbed into the buggy.

Rather than go past the open doors down the loading dock, he turned the buggy in a half circle and went back to the side street. As they waited for a break in the lane of ore wagons, Pete said, "Laurie, I'm leaving your place before I'm asked to leave."

Laurie said quietly, "Yes, I think that's best, Pete." When he found a break in the traffic, Pete drove across the street, heading down the side street. Once on it, he said, "Will you explain to Aunt Martha that I didn't put you in danger, Laurie?"

"Of course," she said in a dull voice.

"Will you let me call on you?"

Laurie thought a moment before answering, "Not right away, Pete. Wait and see how Aunt Martha feels."

"I don't really care how Aunt Martha feels. How do you feel?"

Laurie shook her head. "Too much has happened too fast, Pete. I can't tell you how I feel now, except maybe scared." She looked at him now. "For you, I mean."

"Don't be. There's only one of those fired housemen left after today. I don't think he'll be hunting me out."

"But all those men have friends!" Laurie said vehemently. "They'll take up the fight and then where are you? You aren't safe anywhere or any time. Why don't you leave here while you're still alive?"

"Maybe later, but not now."

"But why not now?" Laurie cried passionately. "Why not ride out tonight? What's keeping you here?"

"I said it before, Laurie, I can't tell you."

"Won't, you mean."

"All right, won't."

They were in front of the boarding house now and Pete reined in. He got out, tied the horse, and came around and handed Laurie down. Together they crossed the veranda and entered the house. Pete halted at the stairs. "I won't come back here, Laurie, until I hear from you."

Still half-angry, Laurie retorted, "Maybe that will be never." They looked at each other in the light cast from the bright lamp on the wall and Pete saw Laurie's lower lip quivering. Whether it was from anger or sadness, Pete didn't know. He said quietly, "Good night, Laurie," and started up the stairs. At the top he turned and surprised Laurie still watching him. When she saw him look at her, she turned and vanished down the corridor.

In his room, Pete gathered up his few belongings, rolled them in his blanket roll and took it out to the buggy. At the livery stable he returned the rig, made his way back to his office and let himself in. Tonight he would sleep on the sofa and tomorrow he would hunt up a cot for, from now on, this was his only home.

10

Around ten o'clock next morning, Maule, with his three bodyguards, came through the doors of the near-empty Crossfire. He gave a "Good morning" to the first two bar-

tenders and before he had reached the third and last bartender, he had come around the end of the bar.

"Morning, Ben," the bartender said. "You got two men
waitin' in the office, Mooney and Wilson. The marshal
stopped by and said he wanted to talk to you. Want me to go
get him?"

Maule, dressed in comfortable range clothes, pursed his
lips in brief thought. "No, Teddy. I'll be with those two all
morning. I'll go see Pete now."

The bodyguards had heard the conversation and now two
of them turned and headed back for the doorway. The third
let Maule precede him.

Late last night, just as he and Lace were about to retire, a
Circle M hand had arrived at the big house at the Circle M
from town with the news of Brisbin's second gun fight of the
day. If Maule had ever wondered if he had hired a tough
marshal yesterday, this proved he had. He wondered what
Pete wanted of him this morning. Surely Pete wouldn't
think it necessary to explain what happened last night. As a
matter of fact, Pete wasn't given to unnecessary explana-
tions of anything he did. More often than not he assumed
his actions explained themselves, and they did.

To get out of the choking dust on this already hot morning, Maule called to the two bodyguards ahead of him to go
through the store. When they entered the big general store it
was oven hot, for the doors were always closed against the
ever-present cloud of street dust. When the bodyguards
came to the closed door which also held a printed sign,
TOWN MARSHAL'S OFFICE, they stepped aside for Maule. He
knocked on the door, was bid enter and opened it.

Pete, seated at the desk, was looking over his shoulder as
Maule entered, and he said, "Morning, Ben." Then he
turned in his chair and looked at the three bodyguards.
"Outside, you three," he said flatly. The bodyguards looked
at Maule, who only nodded, and they filed past him out the
open door that led onto the alley.

Pete waved to the armchair and said, "That's the most comfortable chair, Ben. Sit down."

As he tramped across the room, Maule looked briefly and with approval at the furnishings, and as he sat down in the armchair, he said, "Got everything you need, Pete?"

"Everything except a cot, and Otey is seeing to that."

Maule hadn't missed the blanket roll in the corner and he said, "You aim to sleep here?"

Pete nodded. "After yesterday I'm not exactly welcome at the Mays's boarding house."

"Miss Mays throw you out?"

Pete smiled faintly. "No. I left before she could get around to it."

Maule took a couple of cigars from his breast pocket, tossed one on the desk, bit off the end of the second and put it in his mouth. Pete reached in a drawer for matches and lit both their cigars, then leaned back in his chair.

"You had some day yesterday," Maule observed. "Tell me about last night."

Pete gave a brief account of the fight and of the locking up of Shields. When he described Sheriff Collier's refusal to give him cell keys and how he had handcuffed Shields to the cell bars, Maule let out a great shout of laughter that Pete had to smile at.

"So you rammed it down Collie's throat. Well, well, I don't reckon he liked that even a little bit."

"Not any," Pete agreed. "But I don't know if I've made it stick, Ben. That's what I wanted to talk to you about."

"How's that?"

"Well, Shields is still handcuffed to that cell bar, or at least he was an hour ago. Collier is madder this morning than he was last night, but when he cools down a little, he'll think of taking a hacksaw to those cuffs and Shields will be out."

"Maybe I better talk to him," Maule said.

"Maybe, but you ought to hear this first." Pete went on to tell him of Collier's visit yesterday and of his reaction to the newly passed ordinance and to Pete's frank admission that he never had any intention of becoming the sheriff's partner.

Maule listened carefully to Pete's account of the angry conversation and Collier's veiled threats. Collie, Maule reflected, was getting a little too big for his britches. He had a working accommodation with Collier, but the man's greed was likely to end it. For refusing to cooperate with his town marshal, Maule could ram through an ordinance closing down the sheriff's cribs in the North End town, but that was bound to result in complications.

Pete said, "I think there's a way we can get at him that won't drag you in, Ben. You won't even have to talk to him."

"What is it?"

"Let me take Shields to the county jail at Indian Bend. When I show up with a man charged with attempted murder, they'll ask me why I didn't have him locked up here. And when I tell them Collier refused his jail to me, there'll likely be some hell to pay. Collier might lose his job and with it his string of girls. And you, you had nothing to do with it."

Maule was silent, considering this. No doubt about it, Pete had a head on his shoulders. This was a way to cut Collie down to size and still not involve himself. If Collie was only reprimanded, he would know that he was on a kind of probation; if he was fired, that would be the time for good friend Maule to intercede in his behalf. The county commissioners knew Maule and his position in Banning and they would listen to him. His help would put Collier forever in his debt and serve to check his hunger for more graft money.

"Very pretty, very pretty," Maule said softly. By this time he was smiling. "How did you think that one up, Pete?"

"Why, I guess I was scared into thinking it up. You see, if Shields is loose, I'm apt to get sawed in two with a shotgun. I want him in jail and out of my life."

"Can he travel?"

"In a buckboard, Doc Price says. He's got a leg wound, but no broken bones."

"How long would it take?"

"With good horses, four or five days there and back. Depends how long they keep me at Indian Bend."

Maule nodded as if confirming this in his own mind. "I'll see you get good horses. My own." He tossed his cigar into the cuspidor and rose. "Well, we've got along without a marshal for five years, I guess we can get along without one for five days. Go ahead with it, Pete."

For some strange reason he extended his big hand and Pete, rising, accepted it. "Take care, young fella," Maule said.

Pete nodded. "If my horses are here tomorrow, I'll take off."

Both at noon and suppertime, when Pete accompanied the boy from the restaurant with a tray of food to the cell block, Shields was still handcuffed to the cell bars. Whether from fear of him or Maule, Sheriff Collier had not attempted to free Shields. If Collier would stay away from Shields tonight, then by morning Pete's plan would be in motion.

When dark came, Pete made the rounds of the two saloons. One drunken troublemaker at the Crossfire wanted to take him on at a fist fight, but Pete, not wanting another of his arrests jailed while he was gone, talked the man out of it. Nothing must interfere with his leaving tomorrow.

Because this was Sunday, the saloons closed at eleven, and minutes after that, Pete cruised past the two bars, went to his office, undressed and climbed onto the cot Otey Collins had brought in that afternoon.

As he lay sleepless in the dark, his thoughts turned to Laurie. She would have gone to church today and returned to prepare a big Sunday meal which Moynihan would be too hung-over to eat. Pete discovered that, suddenly deprived of the company of the boarders, he missed them. He even missed Aunt Martha.

He turned over on his side and was hoping for sleep,

when he heard a soft knock on the alley door. Coming off his cot, he pulled on his pants, picked up his gun from the floor beside the cot, then hesitated. The knock came again. He'd be a fool to light the lamp, he knew, for if this was trouble outside, the lamplight would make him a perfect target.

He moved on bare feet across the cool tile floor, lifted the latch, opened the door a crack and said, "Who is it?"

A figure that had been against the wall moved into sight and even in the alley darkness he saw it was a woman.

"It's Lace Ferrill. Let me in, Pete, but don't light the lamp."

Reluctantly Pete swung the door open, a premonition of trouble coming to him. Closing the door again, he said into the darkness, "The sofa's to your right."

"I know."

He heard her move cautiously to the sofa and he himself walked toward his swivel chair and sat down.

"Why the night prowl, Lace? Does Ben know you're here?"

"No, he went out to the ranch. The men took me home and then rode out with him, so don't worry."

"It's you who should be worrying, Lace. Why are you here?"

He heard her sigh in the darkness, then she said, "Ben said you're leaving for Indian Bend tomorrow with a prisoner."

"That's right."

There was another pause and then Lace said with an urgency in her voice, "Take me with you, Pete! Please, oh please take me with you!"

Several questions flashed through Pete's mind and he asked the first one, "Are you trying to trap me, Lace?"

"Trap you? No, I only want help."

"For what?"

"I'm leaving Ben," Lace said quietly, bitterly. "I've had enough, more than enough."

"Then take the stage out."

"Oh, I've tried that. They chase the stage down and take me off it. Then Ben beats me."

"Get a ride with a freighter then."

"I've tried that too. They killed the freighter for hiding me."

Pete said patiently, "Be reasonable, Lace, Ben or one of his crew is going to bring a team and buckboard here tomorrow. Are you going to climb up between me and Shields in front of him?"

"I've thought that out, Pete. This afternoon I got a horse from the feed stable and hid him. As soon as I leave here, I'll take the Indian Bend road. When it gets light I'll pull off the road and wait for you."

"Why not just keep riding?"

"By daylight I'd be recognized. All those freighters and stage drivers know me and they'd get the word back to Ben."

"They'd recognize you with me."

"I don't think so. I'll cover my hair and wear a veil. You see, Bill Shields has a Mexican wife about my size and height. They'll think she's going to Indian Bend to be with him until he's tried."

"Where are you headed for, Lace?"

"I don't know. I've got plenty of money and I can always make a living with cards." She paused. "Please say yes, Pete."

"What do I do when I get back here from Indian Bend and Maule braces me? You've gone and Bill Shields's wife is here. He can add that up too easy."

"Tell him the truth," Lace said. "I flagged you down on the road to Indian Bend. I told you he'd kicked me out, that he was through with me. My horse went lame, you picked me up, just like you'd give anybody a ride when he was afoot in the desert. I didn't tell you where I was going or why."

"Why didn't I turn around and bring you back? That's what he'll ask me."

"Because I told you he'd kicked me out," Lace repeated.

Pete thought about it. Her story was plausible enough and he might get away with it. After all, Maule himself had never warned him away from Lace. The stories of Maule's jealousy of Lace, his absolute possessiveness and his brutalities had all come from Lace herself without Ben's knowledge. Moynihan, of course, had told him of Lace's past, but Maule didn't know that and Moynihan wasn't likely to tell Maule what he'd told Pete about him, for he hated Maule. True, Josh Eddy had told him Lace was Ben's girl and to stay away from her, but nothing more could be read into that than a warning. By a little clever dissembling he could make it appear that by picking up a stranded, discarded Lace, he was doing Maule the greatest of favors in getting her away from him.

His first consideration must be how helping Lace would affect his plans. He didn't see how it could, for when he returned to Banning and volunteered his story of finding Lace to Maule, Lace would be out of the territory and Maule's reach.

"What were you trying to tell me yesterday, Lace?"

"What Ben's done to me. I hoped you could help me without getting killed for it. When Ben said you were taking Shields to Indian Bend, I saw my chance. You will help me, won't you, Pete?"

Remembering her disfiguring scars, the stories of Maule's mistreatment of her, her status as an imprisoned mistress of Maule's, Pete said, "Yes."

11

When Pete, Shields on a crutch beside him, turned into the office alley after breakfast at an upstreet restaurant, the team and buckboard were tied to the loading dock and Maule was sitting on the doorsill, two of his bodyguards leaning against the wall beside him.

As Maule rose, Pete looked at the buckboard with interest, for he had never seen a rig like this before. Metal rods ironed to the four corners of the bed supported tightly stretched canvas. The sides were open but the canvas above would act as a sunshade for the desert crossing.

"Morning, Pete," Maule said. He didn't bother to notice Shields. "All set to go?"

He looked cheerful and unworried and Pete guessed that he had not yet missed Lace. Pete guessed that at this early hour Maule had decided not to wake her. Pete was thankful that they would be out of town before she was missed and that Maule was here to see him leave without her.

"Soon's I get my bedroll, Ben, we're off."

Pete moved past Maule, unlocked the door and was reaching for his blanket roll in the corner, when Maule said, "Why don't I send a couple of men to side you, Pete? You got to sleep sometime and they can guard Shields while you do."

Pete was glad his back was turned to Maule for he felt sure Maule would read the fleeting dismay in his face. When he rose with his blanket roll and turned to Maule, there was a faint smile on his dark face. "You trying to fire me, Ben?"

Maule looked puzzled. "What do you mean, fire you?"

"If word got out that I needed two men to help me guard Shields, I'd be laughed out of this job."

Maule grinned, revealing his even white teeth. "Reckon you would at that."

"If Shields ever had any fighting guts, they were shot out of him the other night. He's about as dangerous as a sick puppy."

Maule nodded. "Just wanted you to know you could have help if you wanted it."

"Thanks, Ben, but I won't need it." Pete pushed past him now, waited for him to come out, locked the door, then moved over to the buckboard. As he passed Shields, he said, "Walk over, I'll help you up."

Shields wasn't a solid man, but now, as he limped over to the buckboard, he seemed shrunken and almost feeble. Pete gave him a boost up onto the wheel hub and watched him settle himself carefully on the buckboard seat, his face tight in a grimace of pain.

Pete untied the team and then climbed in the buckboard, holding the reins. He said, "Like I said, Ben, four or five days."

Ben gave a loose wave of his hand. As Pete put the team in motion, he found that he was sweating, and not from the heat. For the first time since he had agreed to pick up Lace, he wondered if Maule wouldn't put a very simple two and two together. Wouldn't Lace's disappearance and his own trip to Indian Bend appear too coincidental, especially since they both happened on the same day? Of course Williams could report that Lace had come in to Pete's office where they could have planned her escape, Maule would think. But the killing of Becker and wounding of Shields had happened after Lace was in his office and Maule couldn't think his marshal had planned that. The hell with it, Pete thought. Every move he had made in this town had involved a risk, so why not accept this one?

The road to Indian Bend ran north for some miles before it picked up the main east/west road, and for half an hour there was no traffic on it. Afterward, though, they began meeting occasional groups of freighter wagons, whose team-

sters had probably camped together, fed their teams together, harnessed at the same time and left camp at the same
time. The road led through a dusty country of rock, sand,
mesquite and cactus. It was a rough road, sandy when it
wasn't rocky, winding through a broken country whose
earth still held yesterday's heat before it absorbed today's.

They were two hours out when they came to a steep
downgrade where the road had been blasted out to reach the
bottom of the canyon. The pull up the other side was just as
steep and where the road leveled off for the flats again, they
passed through formations of towering red rock. It was here
that Pete heard a shrill whistle off to his right.

Shields, who had been drowsing, now lifted his head and
looked at Pete. "Never heard a bird whistle like that." Pete
looked off to the right and saw a pair of vultures wheeling in
a slow circle in the sky. He reined in the team, which was
blowing hard from the climb out of the canyon.

"We'll blow the horses and wait. Maybe there's somebody
out there."

He had no sooner spoken than Lace appeared around the
base of one of the towering rocks. She was afoot and her
riding outfit of a divided skirt and blouse was black. She
wore a black tricorn hat with a veil folded atop it.

As she came toward them, Shields said, "A woman, by
God!"

"Alone too," Pete said.

As she approached them, she came to a sudden halt,
looked at them and then began to run toward the buckboard, calling, "Pete! Pete Brisbin!"

"My God, it's Lace Ferrill," Shields said.

When Lace came up to the buckboard, Pete wondered
how she would play this and resolved to let her speak first.
Lace halted on Shields's side of the buckboard and said
breathlessly, "Isn't this the damndest thing?"

"What are you doing out here, Lace?" Shields asked.
"Are you alone?"

Lace nodded. "I was on my way to Indian Bend. This

morning, a rattler spooked my horse down there in the canyon. He threw me and the last I saw of him he was galloping up the canyon. I climbed up here to see if I could see him, but he's gone."

So far so good, Pete thought and he asked the question he was sure Shields would ask. "When did you leave Banning?"

"At daylight."

"And you were riding alone?" There was just the right note of incredulity in Pete's question, and at Lace's nod, he said, "Why?"

"Because Ben kicked me out. He's through with me."

Shields turned his head to look at Pete and there was disbelief in his face. Before Shields could open his mouth, Lace went on. "It's a wonderful feeling. No more bodyguards, no spying, no more beatings."

"What's the matter with the stage, Lace?" Shields said. "This is no place for a woman to be traveling alone."

"I couldn't wait to get away from him, Bill. Besides, I was afraid he'd change his mind."

"Well, we can't leave you here," Pete said. "Give her a hand up, Bill."

Shields held out his hand and Lace stepped over his feet and seated herself between them. As Pete extended the canteen to her, Shields said, "What about her horse?"

"He'll make it back to the road and some freighter will pick him up," Pete said. As he watched Lace drink, he admired how she had handled this. If Maule sent a man to Indian Bend to query Shields in jail, he would tell the same story that Pete would have already told Maule. They had taken her at her word and only tried to help her and Maule both.

When Lace had had her drink, she handed back the canteen to Pete, then lowered the black veil over her face and hair and tied it in the back.

"You'd be surprised how this cuts down the glare," she said by way of explanation.

As he put the team in motion, Pete knew that no passing freighter or stage driver could possibly recognize her or even spot her red hair through the veil.

They watered the horses at the first stage relay station and at the second station, a dirty adobe, Pete brought out their tin plates of food to the buckboard, after explaining to the agent that he had a wounded prisoner and his wife with him and that it was too painful for the prisoner to move. The traffic was not a hundredth as heavy as the wagon traffic in Banning, but they passed many freight wagons and three stages.

That evening they reached the third relay station and after Pete reined in, he said, "Want to stretch your legs, Lace, while I fill up the canteens?"

He nudged her with his elbow and she looked at him. "Yes, they're numb."

Pete swung down and Lace moved over and held out her hand. "Catch me if I fall, Pete. I don't think my legs will hold me up." They didn't and Pete caught her under her arms and steadied her. Then he took her elbow and walked her around in a slow circle.

Away from Shields, Pete said, "Follow me."

After she was able to walk, Pete went back to the buckboard, took a rope from its bed and tied one of the horses to the tie rail in front of the adobe station. This was in case Shields had some notion of escape, sick as he was. Then he took the two canteens which were nearly empty and headed for the adobe corral where a thin trickle of water fell from the pipe into the watering trough.

As he was filling the first canteen, Lace came up. "Bill can't hear from here. What is it?" she asked.

"Can you stick it out another night without sleep, Lace?"

"If I have to. Why?"

"We passed three stages today and one has got to be headed for Banning. Ben's already missed you so he'll be checking with the drivers. As soon as the driver reports seeing us, he'll be after us. If we stop for sleep they could catch us."

"But what about our horses? They'll never make it."

"I'll make a deal for fresh horses right here. You finish filling the canteens while I hunt up the agent."

It took Pete twenty minutes to arrange for a fresh team and for the hostler to get them in harness. His badge of office plus the information that he had a very sick wounded prisoner, plus the fact that he was leaving his own horses was enough to clinch the bargain. They were on their way again.

It was full daylight when they arrived at Indian Bend, the county seat. It was built on a bend of the *Rio Conejos* that was dry two-thirds of the year, but the big cottonwoods that they had seen half an hour before reaching town attested to a good supply of subsurface water. As they drove down the main street, Pete saw the new brick courthouse looming over one-story adobe buildings and warehouses. This was a commercial town and a cow town, Pete judged, for the mountains to the north were timbered and where there was timber, there was grass, and this would be the trading center for the country to the north.

By agreement, Pete's first chore was to hunt up the stage station and put Lace on the first stage west. Pete found the station, which consisted of one room with a feed stable whose corrals stretched back to the banks of the dry river.

Pete reined in the team, handed Lace down and went with her into the station through whose window he could keep an eye on Shields.

Pete inquired of the sallow young man behind the counter about stage times and found that the teams were making up the first stage west, due to leave within the half hour. From the purse at her belt Lace paid for the fare to San Diego and then she turned to face Pete. "Tell Ben it was San Francisco, Pete."

Pete nodded. "But don't make it that, Lace. You'll walk into trouble there."

Lace smiled faintly. "I already have," she said, and then extended her hand. As Pete accepted it, she moved toward him and kissed him on the cheek, then she backed away and looked at him. "Ever since I was fifteen, I was sure I wouldn't live to meet a decent man. I was wrong. Thank you for everything."

"Keep your head down, Lace, and luck to you." He turned and started for the door and then halted abruptly and came back to her. "Favor for favor, Lace. Did Ben ever tell you he was an army deserter?"

Lace nodded. "So that explains you."

"That's it," Pete said. "Good luck."

12

When Lace had not shown up at the Crossfire by eleven in the morning, Maule began to wonder about her absence. Midnight was not a late hour for her to retire and she should be up and around at this hour, and if she were, she should have dropped by before this. He thought of sending for his horse but by the time it was sent for, saddled and delivered, he could be at Lace's place.

Accordingly, he picked up his bodyguard in the corridor, went out of the back door of the Crossfire, tramped down the alley past the Mays's boarding house, took a right and a left and walked along the block where Lace's one-story adobe house lay among tall cottonwoods, his bodyguards ahead of him and behind him.

At the open gate which opened on to a garden-bright patio, he didn't even have to tell his men to wait at the gate. If Lace was still sleeping he didn't want to wake her, so he headed across the patio to the kitchen wing directly ahead, where Carmelita, Lace's cook and housekeeper, was usually found to be working.

Entering the kitchen, he found Carmelita at her ironing. She was only a girl and a very pretty Mexican one and young enough to have learned to speak and understand English in this mainly English-speaking camp. To her, "Good morning, Señor Maule," Ben gave a pleasant nod and asked, "Where's Miss Ferrill, Carmelita?"

"I don't know for sure, Señor. She has went out. Not here."

"Did she have breakfast here?"

"No, Señor. Sometimes no, sometimes yes, but not this morning."

Maule frowned. "Did she sleep here?"

"Oh yes, Señor. I made up her bed."

So she had slept here last night but Carmelita hadn't seen her this morning. That was unusual, but Lace, as he was the first to know, had odd whims and fancies that were unpredictable. He said then, "Come with me, Carmelita," and went outside and cut diagonally across the patio and entered the furthermost room of the other wing which was Lace's bedroom. He stepped inside, Carmelita following, and looked about him. Besides the big bed, scattered easy chairs and her dresser, there was a huge ceiling-high walnut wardrobe that served as Lace's clothes closet. Walking over to it, Maule swung both doors open. There was a full-length mirror on the back of each and ahead of him a rack of dresses, shoes below them, hats on a shelf above. Maule turned to Carmelita and said, "See what's missing, will you?"

"Missing?"

Maule said testily, "She didn't go out naked. What was she wearing? And what did she take with her?"

"Ah, *si.*" Carmelita moved past him and then began to tap each dress and coat and suit one after the other. When she was finished she stepped back, knelt down and looked at the line of shoes. Finished with them, her glance briefly scanned the line of hats before she turned and said, "She must be riding, Señor. Black hat, black shirt and black boots are not here. Everything else here."

Ben felt a wave of relief followed by a feeling of irritation. He didn't like having Lace ride alone, but she had told him that if he insisted on sending one of his men with her, she would not ride at all. That would destroy the pleasure of being alone. In exchange for her promise always to ride within sight of the camp and always on his Circle M horse, he had given in, but last night, when they had parted, she had not asked for a horse.

An uneasiness touched him now, but he only said, "Good girl," to Carmelita and turned and went out. At the gate, he said to the tallest of his bodyguards, "Bring the horses over to the Crossfire, Beach, and ask if Miss Ferrill rented a horse or rig today."

Back at the Crossfire, Maule left his bodyguards out in the corridor and shut his office door. After opening the windows against the oppressive heat of the day, he began to pace a restless circle around the room. This heat should have driven Lace back to the house long since. The fact that it hadn't and that she hadn't asked him to send her a horse pointed to several things. One was the possibility that someone had driven her somewhere and it would be a secret somewhere. The fact that she had taken only the riding outfit she wore and left all of her personal belongings at home indicated she planned to return. The time she had tried to escape by stage she had taken a valise, just as when she had tried to escape under the tarpaulin of a freighter's wagon. Was this another escape attempt? Had she purposely left all her clothes except what she wore in order to mislead him? There were no answers to these questions—yet.

When the knock came on the door, Maule was close to his desk and he sat down and said, "Yes."

The door opened and Beach stepped in. "The horses are here, Ben, but there's somethin' else. Lace got a horse from the feed stable around suppertime last night."

"Last night?" Maule echoed. He felt a wild wrath rise up

in him. How could that be? Carmelita had said her bed had been slept in. Was Carmelita lying? Reluctantly he had to admit to himself that it was very easy to muss up a bed to make it look as if it had been slept in. So Lace had a whole night's start on him if she was bent on escape.

Maule thought about this while Beach watched him. Lace couldn't be traveling alone, Maule thought. Reckless as she was, she knew the odds of survival were nil if she took off cross-country. If she clung to the roads, as she would have to do, someone who knew her would see her and report it to him.

Maule came to his decision then and rose. He passed Beach, who turned and followed him. In the corridor Maule said, "Back to the feed stable," to the bodyguard.

When they pulled up before the arch of the stable runway, Maule said, "Beach, go find the hostler that gave Lace the horse."

Beach dismounted and returned a few moments later with a doltish-looking young man wearing filthy clothes. He halted and looked at the three mounted men.

"You the one that hired out a horse to a red-haired lady yesterday suppertime?"

"Yup. She give me ten dollars."

"For you or for the horse?"

"For me to keep, she said."

"When you were hired, didn't they tell you not to hire out a horse or a rig to a red-haired woman?"

"There's more than one red-haired woman here."

Maule raised his glance to an elderly bald man now standing in the archway. "I told him," the man said.

Maule nodded and said, "All right, boys."

Lefty and his companion swung out of their saddles, moved over to the hostler and each took an arm. Beach was already taking off his brass-studded belt and wrapping it around the palm of his left hand as he moved out in front of the hostler who, finally comprehending, began to struggle.

What happened then was almost surgical in its precision.

With his right hand Beach worked on the hostler's unprotected belly while with his belt-wrapped left hand he worked on the hostler's face. Within minutes the hostler, mouth mashed and nose flattened and face savaged, was freed and fell unconscious in the dust.

Beach crossed over to the watering trough and began to rinse the blood from his belt. Maule looked at the bald man in the stable archway. "Let that happen again, Johnny, and I'll burn you out and shoot your horses."

"I hear you," the bald man said.

Now Maule said, "Lefty, go check the stage office."

Since the stage office was next to the feed stable, Lefty walked the short distance and vanished through an open doorway. Beach had rinsed his belt and put it back on and was mounting his horse when Lefty returned and was halted by Maule.

"No women passengers on either stage goin' out, he says."

"Did the drivers coming in meet a woman on the road?"

"He never asked because he didn't know Lace was gone. He says if they had, though, they'd sure of told him. He's goin' to ask the driver of the last stage due around four. He'll send us word."

That left only the freighting outfits to check, and that would be more difficult. Still, most of the teamsters for the regular freight outfits timed their trips so they would reach the camp in midafternoon in time to unload by dark so they'd have an early start in the morning.

Maule looked at the two stablehands who had come out to take the unconscious hostler back into the stable, but he really didn't see them. He was thinking of the best way to go about this. When he had it, he said to his patiently waiting men, "Lefty, you and Roy get something to eat, then find some shade out on the north road. Stop every freight wagon and ask the teamsters if they saw a woman on the road. Stop all stages and riders too. Lefty, you do the talking. If you pick up anything, have Roy bring it to me at the office."

Back in his office, Beach on guard outside, Maule sent a bartender out for some food and when it came he ate alone. All through the meal that he wolfed, and afterward, he kept telling himself that something, some trail of Lace, was bound to turn up. She'd tried before and he'd caught her before and he was smarter than she was.

It was after four o'clock and Maule was talking with Josh Eddy in Eddy's office when Lefty, Roy and a bearded, to-bacco-chewing, roughly dressed man stepped through the door. Lefty said, "Got it," and thumbed toward the bearded man.

"Hello, Tom," Maule said. He was a stage driver and Maule knew him. "Let's have it."

"I seen this rig comin' at me and I knew it was yours because I never seen another like it. There was three of 'em —a woman between two men. I couldn't tell who was drivin' but I thought I knew the other man. He used to work right here."

"Bill Shields," Maule said grimly. "Did you recognize the woman?"

"Nope. I only got a quick look and she had a veil on. But at the next relay station—Armstead's—they told me it was the marshal takin' a prisoner and his wife to the Indian Bend jail."

Maule's glance shifted. "Roy, go see if Shields's Mex wife is home. Make it quick." He returned his attention to the stage driver as Roy went out. "What time was this?"

"Around noon."

Maule cussed softly. He reached in a pocket, pulled out an eagle, rose and handed it to the stage driver. "Buy yourself a drink, Tom. Thanks." The driver went out and Maule said to Lefty and Beach, "Stay here."

He crossed the corridor to his office and closed the door, then moved to his desk and sat down. He was certain it was Lace Tom had seen, which meant that Pete Brisbin had betrayed him. But did it? His quarrel with the sheriff over jailing Shields wasn't a fake; too many people had seen

Shields handcuffed to the cell bars, and Pete's trip to Indian Bend to jail Shields was reasonable. Had he just picked her up on the road? Where was her horse? He didn't know now but he would eventually.

One thing was certain—he had to find Lace and Brisbin and bring them back. Not he himself, of course. He had never been to Indian Bend, with its Army post across the river. Some old trooper might recognize him.

A knock came on the door and then it was opened. Roy, hand still on the knob said, "His wife's here, Ben. I saw her."

Maule said, "Send Beach and Lefty in."

When they came in and stood before his desk, he said grimly, "Lefty, you and Beach are in for a hell of a ride. I want you to take off for Indian Bend right now. Ride all night. Pick up fresh horses at the relay stations. I want Lace back and Brisbin with her. Now get going. Get some money from Josh before you leave."

13

The office of the sheriff of Mesilla County was in the basement of the new brick courthouse and Shields, more than half sick and without sleep since they had left Banning, had to be helped down the stairs. The sheriff's office was immediately at the foot of the stairs, its door open, and when Pete with Shields's arm around his neck and carrying Shields's crutch entered the room, the sheriff, who had heard their slow descent, came out of his chair, his mouth open in surprise. He was a tall, white-haired man gone to fat and he didn't offer to help Pete with Shields as they crossed the room to the chair by the sheriff's desk.

Pete eased the groaning Shields into the chair, propped the crutch against the wall beside him and then introduced himself by saying, "Sheriff Humphrey, I'm Pete Brisbin, the new marshal at Banning. I've got a prisoner for you."

They shook hands and Pete saw the surprise mingled with distaste in the sheriff's meaty face. No law officer, Pete knew, welcomed a prisoner, because they had to be fed and taken care of. Especially they didn't welcome a sick or wounded prisoner.

Pete went on, "This is Bill Shields, Sheriff. He's charged with attempted murder."

The sheriff nodded to Shields and, perplexed, asked, "Why bring him to me? You've got a jail in Banning."

"I know, but Deputy Sheriff Collier refused to lock him up."

"Now wait a minute. If he did that he must have had some doubts about the charge."

"He might have, but I don't, Sheriff. It was me he tried to murder."

"Well, now," the sheriff said slowly. He pointed to a straight-back chair against the side wall. "Pull up a chair and tell me about it." He sat down in his own chair while Pete brought a chair over and sat down facing him. When he was seated, Sheriff Humphrey said, "Now what happened?"

Pete told about the attempted bushwhack, the killing of Becker and wounding and capture of Shields and Deputy Sheriff Collier's contention that this was a town matter, not a county matter, and of his refusal to jail Shields.

When he was finished, the sheriff observed in a noncommittal voice, "You and him don't like each other much, do you? Why?"

"Maybe you better get that from him," Pete said and stood up. "You'll want me to sign something, won't you?"

"Like a complaint against Collie?" the sheriff asked, not bothering to hide the dislike in his voice.

"Nothing like that. He's your deputy. Do what you want with him. I mean a charge."

"We call it a complaint. Sure." He pulled open a drawer in the flat-topped desk, pulled out a printed form, filled in the cause of complaint with a pen whose nib was caked with ink from never having been cleaned, and then extended the pen to Pete. After signing, Pete laid the pen on the desk and straightened up. "Now, if you'll give me a receipt for the prisoner, I'll be on my way."

"We never give a receipt for a prisoner unless he's brought in from out of the territory," the sheriff said in a surly tone of voice.

"You do this time," Pete said mildly. "I want a receipt and you'll give it to me."

The two men stared at each other for a long moment and then the sheriff shrugged, drew a blank piece of paper from the desk drawer and as he was dipping the pen into the ink well, said, "How do you spell those names, yours and his?"

Pete told him, received the receipt, read it, folded it, put it in his pocket, said, "Goodbye," without offering to shake hands and left the courthouse. As he drove the buckboard back down the main street on the way to the feed stable, he wondered what chain of events the deposit of Shields here would set off. Obviously, the sheriff wanted to protect Collier, but could he? It really didn't matter, Pete thought, because Shields was only an excuse to get here.

At the feed stable, he turned his tired team over to the hostler with orders to grain the team and grease the axles of the buckboard. Afterward, he went into the stage-line office where the clerk came up to meet him across the counter. It was the same clerk who had sold Lace her ticket. Pete asked, "The young lady get off on the stage?"

"Sure did."

"The San Francisco stage made up yet?"

"Why, it's gone, mister. They both leave about the same time. You never asked, so I never told you."

Pete drew an eagle from his pocket and laid it on the counter. The clerk looked at the eagle and then back at him.

"I'm trying to tell you, you've missed it," the clerk said.

"I know. But if anybody asks you which stage the lady took, it was the one for San Francisco. Have you got that?"

"Is somebody looking for her?"

"Maybe they will be, but she took the San Francisco stage." He gestured to the gold coin on the counter. "Don't put that in the till. Put it in your pocket."

Grinning, the clerk picked up the coin and said, "I'm dead certain it was the San Francisco stage. Thank you, sir."

Afoot now, and purposely, for whoever came for Lace would wonder about his renting a horse, he headed for the long wooden bridge that crossed the river midway between the feed stable and the courthouse. Once across it, and having climbed the gentle rise to the flats beyond, he saw the cluster of adobe buildings, sheds and corrals that made up Fort Lyman.

Even at this distance, Pete could spot the flag waving gently in the morning breeze, a sight that always warmed him and brought back a host of bittersweet memories. As he drew closer he could see that the post, made up mainly of single-story adobe buildings, followed the usual pattern of post buildings, facing each other across the long rectangular parade ground. The stables, corrals, warehouses and feed barns lay immediately to the south, for the prevailing west winds would keep the odor and flies away from the living quarters. The center gate faced the north, and as Pete swung off the road on the short approach to it, he could not help but remark that one of the houses he could see through the white gate was almost a replica of the house he and Anne were billeted in at Fort Ely. Bare and sparsely furnished as they inevitably were, they housed his kind of people and he wondered if the young wives living here had been as appalled as Anne had been when they were assigned married officers' quarters.

Why, he wondered suddenly, did it take the sight of a

cavalry post to remind him of Anne? Here it was again and he felt ashamed. It was as if thoughts of Laurie and the violence of these past days had blacked out all thoughts of Anne, and this was not right.

At the sentry gate, Pete said to the trooper whose station this was, "Who's your commanding officer, Trooper?"

"Major Henderson, sir. You'll find him in the building where the flag's flying."

"I know," Pete said dryly.

Headquarters building was to his right, and at the tie rail in front of it, Pete saw a pair of horses tied, the brand U.S. plain on their hips. At the far end of the parade ground mounted drill was being held and over the shouted commands Pete could hear the crackle of gunfire, undoubtedly coming from the rifle butts beyond.

Pete crossed the *portal* and entered past the open door of the headquarters building and was immediately in the officer-of-the-day's room with its inevitable clerk behind the regulation desk. Pete gave the scholarly looking corporal a "Good day," and said, "I'd like to see Major Henderson, Corporal."

The corporal rose slowly and said, "He's with the officer-of-the-day now, but he won't be long. Who will I say is asking for him?"

It was on the tip of Pete's tongue to tell him it was Lieutenant Brisbin, but he thought better of it, knowing that at the next mess call his unexplained appearance in civilian clothes would be post gossip. "Pete Brisbin," he said.

The corporal went around his desk to the closed door in the wall to the left, knocked, got a summons and went inside, closing the door behind him.

In less than a minute a second lieutenant came out, nodded civilly to Pete and went over to the second desk. The corporal halted in the doorway and said, "Come in, Mr. Brisbin."

From force of habit, Pete took off his hat, tucked it under

his left arm and moved past the corporal, who closed the door behind him.

Major Henderson's desk was beside the window looking out onto the parade ground. The major was not seated in his chair; he was standing in the middle of the room, hands on hips, observing his visitor. He was a lean little terrier of a man with curly gray-shot black hair, and the puzzled glance in his gray eyes was now on the marshal's badge pinned to Pete's shirt.

Pete came to attention, saluted and said, "Lieutenant Peter Brisbin, sir."

The major's glance lifted from the badge to Pete's face. "You mean ex-Lieutenant, don't you?"

"No, sir. I'm on detached service, sir, from I troop, Third Cavalry, Fort Ely, Major Horton commanding."

There was a long uncomfortable silence and finally the major said, "I hear what you're saying, Brisbin, but I've never seen an officer of the United States Cavalry wearing that badge. Are you a marshal or are you a cavalry officer? You can't be both."

"May I sit down, sir," Pete asked.

Major Henderson nodded and pointed to the armchair facing the desk. Pete moved over to the desk and at the same time reached in his pocket and drew out a knife. Opening it, he put it on the desk, then leaned over and pulled off his right boot. Holding it in his lap, he took the knife and began cutting. Curious as to what was going on, the major came over and watched him.

Before leaving Fort Ely, Pete had had the post cobbler fashion a pocket which he had sewn on the inside of Pete's right boot. After identification papers and his orders were placed in the pocket, the cobbler had sewn it tightly shut for protection against weather and accidental discovery.

Now Pete cut the waxed thread at the top of the pocket, took out the papers, put his boot back on and rose. "These are my orders, sir, and identification."

Major Henderson unfolded the papers that Pete offered

and studied them carefully. Finished, he smiled, held out his hand and said, "It's good to meet you, Lieutenant. Major Horton writes that you will tell me the nature of your assignment."

"It'll take some time, sir, but it will explain why I'm wearing this badge."

Major Henderson went around his desk, still carrying the papers, sat down and gestured for Pete to take the chair. Pete seated himself and began talking, beginning with the killing of the paymaster and his detail headed for Camp Stambaugh seven years ago. As he told of his efforts to get close to Ben Maule and of finally being appointed Maule's marshal, a look of incredulity came into Major Henderson's face, although at the same time he was smiling. Pete finished with an account of Lace's escape.

When he finished, Major Henderson shook his head. "So Sergeant Fairly has been right under our noses all this time."

Pete nodded, and returned to the subject of the contents of the company clerk's letter to Major Horton. "Even if you knew the man, you'd never lay eyes on him, sir. When your troopers show up in Banning, he drifts south across the border."

"Well, how do you propose to snatch him away from these men you say are always with him?"

"That's why I'm here, Major. Suppose you send a detail into Banning with the news that you are looking for troopers who deserted last week, and suppose you sent a second detail to watch the road that runs south of Banning to the border. Maule's reaction to the arrival of the first detail would be to run. He's afraid of being identified by some old trooper who'd recognize him. Then he'd run into your second detail south of town and we'd have him."

"There'd be a fight, of course," the major said.

Pete nodded. "I expect there would. You can't ask your men who're being shot at not to shoot back, but we want Maule alive."

The major frowned now. "That's a large order, isn't it?"

"Too large maybe, but let me ask you, sir. Do you go along with the idea of the two details?" At Major Henderson's nod, Pete went on. "Do you have in mind the officer who'd lead the second detail?"

The major answered promptly. "Yes. You passed him on your way in here. Lieutenant Blanton. Why?"

"Give him a good look at me, sir, because I'll be riding next to Maule when he sees me next."

"Can you guarantee that?" the major asked skeptically. "According to your story you helped his girl escape."

"I'll be riding beside him, even if I'm his prisoner. And I'm likely to be one."

"Isn't it safer for you to go along with Blanton and point out your man?"

"Maybe safer, but if I don't show up in Banning on schedule, Maule may suspect what I've been up to and run."

Henderson sighed, then rose, crossed the room, opened the door and said, "Lieutenant Blanton, please come in."

When the young lieutenant stepped into the room, Pete rose and Major Henderson introduced them. When Pete was introduced as Lieutenant Brisbin, Blanton's lean face under its cap of blond hair showed no surprise but only a reserved friendliness.

"Mr. Blanton, take a good look at Lieutenant Brisbin. You'll be seeing him again in a few days time and I want you to recognize him."

"Yes, sir," Blanton said. He looked at Pete fullface and then made a slow circle of him, noting profile and height, then he said, "Would you put your hat on, Lieutenant?"

After Pete had done so, Blanton circled him again, then turned to Henderson and said, "I'll recognize him, sir."

Henderson nodded. "I'll tell you what this is all about later." He waited until Blanton had left the room, then returned to his chair and, sitting down, said, "He's a good man. His promotion should come through any day now."

He leaned forward, arms on the desk, and said, "Describe this country where he'll have to hide his men."

Pete gave him a description of the canyon he had traveled paralleling the road to Circle M. He warned about the tell-tale dust which would give away the presence of other horses, so he recommended a dismounted action.

He also recommended that both detachments travel cross-country and not by road, where news of their movements would be carried by every stage driver who passed them and thus forewarn of their coming. He then suggested that the first detachment should enter Banning on the morning of the third day, counting tomorrow as the first day. The second detachment should be in place that same morning.

When he was finished, Major Henderson said, "Anything else?"

"One more thing, sir," Pete said. "Your detail that goes into Banning should be made up of the oldest troopers on the post. That will flush out Maule quicker than anything you can do. He'll figure that any man who has served two or three enlistments in the Cavalry could have known him."

Pete rose and Major Henderson rose with him, saying dryly, "Well, Marshal, you've got your job cut out for you," and extended his hand. "Good luck, and my men will be off at dawn."

He escorted Pete to the door, said, "Goodbye," and before Pete was out of the day room, Major Henderson called, "Come inside, Mr. Blanton."

A wind had come up that was oven hot while Pete had been with Henderson and as he walked back into Indian Bend he could feel the blasting heat on his back.

At the feed stable, spotting the hostler out in the back by the corral, he tramped down the dark stallway and asked the hostler to harness his team to the buckboard. He stepped back into the shade of the stable and was watching the hostler at work when he heard someone behind him. Before he could turn, he felt the barrel of a gun jammed in his back, while at the same time his own gun was lifted from its holster. Turning then, he saw Lefty and Beach.

Lefty, still holding the gun, said mockingly, "Why, if it ain't the marshal of Banning. We're here after a stolt buckboard, Marshal."

"What's the gun for?" Pete asked.

"Just a way to get yours," Beach said.

"If you're looking for Lace, she's gone," Pete said.

"That's right. On the way to San Francisco, she is," Lefty said. Then he asked tonelessly, "Why'd you give her a ride?"

"Was I supposed to leave her out in the desert?"

"You were supposed to bring her back," Beach said roughly.

Pete looked from one to the other and from the expression in their faces and their tone of voice knew pretty much how Maule was going to greet him.

"If I told you what really happened, you wouldn't believe me, would you?" Pete asked.

"No," Beach said.

"It wouldn't be what really happened," Lefty said.

"All right, I won't even try. Let's take a walk to the courthouse and you two have a talk with Bill Shields."

"Go ahead and tell us," Lefty said.

"Damned if I will," Pete said quietly. "You'll get the story from him."

Lefty and Beach looked at each other. Pete asked sardonically, "What are you going to say to Ben when he asks if my story jibed with Bill's?"

There was pure hatred in Lefty's bleak eyes as he said, "Lead the way."

They didn't speak on the way to the courthouse, where they found Sheriff Humphrey in the basement office. Pete said to the sheriff, "These two men want to talk to the prisoner I brought in, Sheriff."

"All right." Humphrey looked at the three of them, shrugged and said, "Leave your guns on my desk." He rose, took the set of cell keys from the nail over the desk and waited while Lefty deposited his and Pete's gun on the desk and Beach put down his own.

Out in the corridor the sheriff unlocked the heavy wooden door, then led the way into the six-cell jail.

"You want inside?" he asked over his shoulder.

"No," Pete answered.

Bill Shields was in the last cell on the right and was sitting on his cot waiting for whatever came next. He had been sleeping, Pete knew, but when he saw Lefty and Beach his face came alert.

The sheriff said, "Knock, when you want out," and left them. When he had closed the door, Pete said, "Bill, tell Lefty and Beach how we met Lace."

"You keep out of this," Lefty said curtly. To Bill he said, "All right, Bill, how did you?"

Bill told about their being whistled at after they had come out of the canyon and of Pete pulling up the team because he thought somebody might be in trouble. He said how they were surprised to see Lace walk out from the rocks and how she first told them of being thrown from her horse.

"Did she say why she was there?" Lefty interrupted.

"Sure. She said Maule had booted her out."

"Did you believe that?" Beach said.

"Why, hell, yes," Shields said flatly. "If he hadn't booted her out what was she doing there alone without a couple of you siding her?"

"If Ben booted her out why didn't she take a stage?" Lefty asked.

"She said she was afraid he'd change his mind and she wanted to get away from him."

Now Lefty looked at Pete who was leaning against the cell bars, his arms folded across his chest. "Why did you drive all night if you thought Ben had got rid of her? What was your hurry?"

"Two reasons," Pete said. He nodded in Shields's direction. "He already tried to bushwhack me once. Do you think I'd camp out with him or sleep in a relay station and have him try it again? I'd have gone straight through even if Lace hadn't been with us."

"What was the other reason?" Lefty asked.

"Lace. Lice in all the blankets and food that would gag a dog."

"You knew damn well she was trying to escape. She's tried it three or four times before."

"Now, who would tell me that?" Pete asked dryly. "Maule never said so, Beach never said so, you never said so. I've only been in this country a week and I'm no mind reader."

"You're lying," Lefty said. The words were scarcely out of his mouth before Pete backhanded him a blow across his mouth. Lefty staggered across the walkway between the cells and was brought up by the bars of the cell opposite. His hand instinctively dove for his gun and touched only an empty holster.

Beach brought both hands up in a move to take off his brass-studded belt. Pete stepped back now, his hand going into his pocket for the knife that he hoped would again save his knuckles from breaking. With his left arm, he reached through the bars for Shields's crutch which was propped against the wall at the foot of the cot. Pulling the crutch through the bars, he grasped it close to its tip, its mallet head pointed toward Beach, and began his slow advance. Lefty was against the jail bars, watching. Beach began to back up to give himself time to wrap the belt round his fist.

When Pete was even with Lefty, he knew he couldn't risk going further and exposing his back. With a surprise back-handed motion, he swung the crutch, not at Beach, but at Lefty's head. The thick armrest of the crutch was parallel to the floor so that it was in effect a long-handled hammer. Pete's swing drove the armrest into Lefty's temple. Too late, Lefty started to raise his hands to ward off the blow and then they ceased moving. Lefty's knees bent and he pitched face down, unconscious before his head rapped the stone of the floor.

Pete stepped over Lefty now and confronted Beach, whose hands were in front of his belly just finishing wrapping the belt around his fist. Using a side-arm motion, Pete again swung the crutch, aiming for Beach's left arm. It was a savage blow that found its mark with such violence that the shaft of the crutch splintered. Pete drove in now watching Beach's belt-wrapped left hand, hoping that the blow had temporarily damaged it. As he moved in, he saw the left arm fall to Beach's side, powerless, and then Pete was on him.

It was a short and savage fight that was almost no fight at all, for in effect Pete was fighting a one-armed man. He knocked down Beach's guard, drove two swift blows into the midriff which kept the guard down, and then sent a looping swing into Beach's jaw.

Beach staggered back, and as he caromed off the cell bars, Pete swarmed on him. Pete's next to last blow landed on Beach's jaw and drove his head back against the bars. Beach's eyes were unfocused when Pete's last blow sent him sprawling.

Pete paused a moment, looking at the two men, getting his breath, and then moved down the corridor to knock on the plank door.

When the door was opened by Sheriff Humphrey, Pete walked through and passed him. Humphrey stood motionless, looking at the two men on the walkway floor.

"What happened?" Humphrey asked.

"Why, they were fixing to beat me up," Pete said. "One was going to hold me and the other cut me up with that belt around his fist."

Humphrey started in for the cell block but Pete touched his arm. "I think you better leave them there till we have a talk, Sheriff."

Humphrey nodded, came back, locked the corridor door and Pete followed him inside the office.

When the sheriff was seated, Pete standing, Pete asked, "What's the charge for assaulting a law officer, Sheriff?"

"Were you arresting them and were they resisting you?"

"No to both."

"Why, then plain assault," Sheriff Humphrey said.

"That's bailable isn't it?" At the sheriff's nod, Pete said, "Well, they'll have bail money and money to pay their fines. Could you keep them off my back for a day?"

"I'll take them before the judge at eleven o'clock tomorrow. That suit you?"

"Just right," Pete said. He walked over to the desk, picked up his gun and the other two. "Tell them I'll turn over their weapons at Banning." Pete held out his hand. "Thanks for the help, Sheriff."

The sheriff rose, accepted his hand. "I'm glad you don't hit town often, Marshal, but I'm always glad to help you."

Within fifteen minutes, Pete had collected the carbines from the saddle scabbards of Beach and Lefty's saddles at the stable, and they lay alongside the two pistols in the bed of the buckboard as he drove his relay team out of Indian Bend for Banning.

14

When Moynihan came in for supper the evening Lefty and Beach left town, Laurie saw that he was a little drunk and bursting with news. As he sat down, he announced to his table and the other, "Well, our lady gambler at the Crossfire has flew the coop along with our brand new marshal."

Laurie was filling coffee cups at Moynihan's table and now she looked at Moynihan and said, "You mean they went away together?"

"They didn't start out together, but they met on the stage road." As the boarders passed the platters of food to him, Moynihan told the story that he and Ames Williams had pieced together but would never print. The reason for Maule's men beating the hostler wasn't hard to come by. He had rented Lace a horse on which, during the night, she had headed out for Indian Bend. The rest of the story, Moynihan said, came from old Tom, the stage driver who had seen Lace in Maule's buckboard with Pete Brisbin driving. Lefty and Beach were seen riding out of town, presumably to overtake the buckboard and bring Lace back.

Laurie listened to this in stunned disbelief before she recovered herself, poured Moynihan's coffee and returned to the kitchen. Laughter came from the dining room as Moynihan speculated as to how the romance had been carried on and the escape planned and carried out, and Laurie found herself hating him. True, she did not know all Pete's movements after that terrible night of the alley gun fight, but how could he have had time to court Lace and plan their escape together? Her hopes told her that Pete couldn't have run off with this gambling hussy, who was secondhand at best, but the facts said he had.

She heard the chairs scraping in the dining room and the murmur of conversation recede down the hall. Aunt Martha had heard none of this and Laurie supposed she would have to tell her, but not now.

Moynihan had not finished eating and after clearing the other table, she started in clearing his. "Well, what do you make of your Pete Brisbin, Laurie?"

"He's not my Pete Brisbin, and I make of it just what you do," Laurie said calmly.

"That sure was a short spell to serve as marshal. He barely got the badge warmed up."

"Well, if he marries her and brings her back as his wife, what can Ben Maule do?"

When Moynihan, his mouth full, did not answer immediately, Laurie waited until he had swallowed. The first thing he did then was laugh derisively. "He won't marry her and he won't be back. We've seen the last of both of them."

Watching him, Laurie asked, "Aren't you just guessing?"

Moynihan regarded her with pity, as he would observe a retarded child. "I think Maule would kill them both, but him for sure. His men are out to kill them now."

"That's only saloon gossip," Laurie said. She could hear the quaver in her own voice and she saw that Moynihan caught it too.

"You liked him," Moynihan said.

"So did you."

Moynihan nodded. "At first, yes. When he took that marshal's badge, I changed my mind. Why didn't you?"

"How do you know I didn't? He's not living here, is he?"

"How's your coffee?" Moynihan asked.

Laurie left with an armful of dishes, returned to the dining room and refilled Moynihan's cup.

"What do you really know about him, Laurie?"

"Next to nothing, I guess."

"Then add up what we both know about him. He was a brawler, a killer, a gunman and he was power-hungry. Now he's run off with his boss's woman so we better add treachery to the list."

As Moynihan gulped down his coffee, Laurie was thinking over what he had just said. It was an accurate enough list and added up only to minuses. But there were some pluses too, like his kindness, his thoughtfulness, his gentleness and his humor. They didn't outweigh the minuses, she had to admit.

Moynihan put down his cup and rose. "Forget him, Laurie. He's just something that never happened to us."

Laurie thought she detected a note of bitterness in his voice and she watched him go out. Could it be that Moynihan felt a touch of the same desolation she was feeling? she wondered.

Back in the kitchen, as she helped her aunt clean up the dishes, she told her what Moynihan had told the boarders.

When she finished, Aunt Martha was silent a long while. Then she said, "Well, there was some good in him, Laurie, but I guess we're the only ones who ever saw any of it."

15

The first night out from Indian Bend, Pete spent in the clean bunkhouse of a relay station and slept as if drugged. It was at the next relay station that he returned his team and retrieved his original horses that were now well rested.

He wondered about many things that hot midday as he passed freight wagons and let a stage pass him. For instance, would Lefty and Beach, freed this morning, try to get to Maule ahead of him? With his head start it was improbable that they could, but he really didn't care. What troubled him some was the correct plan of action when he reached Banning. If he went to Maule immediately to tell him he had picked up Lace, this would undercut what he had already told Beach and Lefty and what they would repeat to Maule. After all, the picking up of a woman Maule had discarded could not be classed as news and he should treat it as a trivial thing, not reporting it to Maule immediately but not hiding it either.

It was after dark when he pulled up in the alley by his office. He unlocked the door, lighted the lamp, put his blanket roll in the corner and the confiscated weapons on his desk, then, leaving the door open, he drove the team down to the livery stable. After leaving instructions to wash down the dusty buckboard, rub down and grain the horses, he started back for his office. On the corner, he put his back to the wall of a dark store building and watched the feed stable. It was perhaps three minutes before he saw a stableman come through the stable doorway and cut up the street toward the Crossfire at a fast walk. The news of his return would be out in less than a minute and he headed back for his office.

There he found Sheriff Collier seated on the sofa. He greeted Pete with the darkest of scowls.

"Get your man locked up?" Collier asked.

"That's what I went for," Pete said easily.

"What did Humphrey say when you brought Shields in?"

"Why, he was too surprised to say much," Pete said. He walked over and sat down and swiveled his chair to face Collier.

"You told him I wouldn't jail Bill, of course?"

"Of course."

"What did he say?"

"Only that we mustn't like each other much. I told him he better ask you about that."

"Was he mad?"

Pete only nodded. He could have added that the sheriff was mad at him, not at Collier, but he didn't.

"Well, I only done what I thought was right and I'd do it again."

"I wonder if you will," Pete said mildly.

Then Pete heard what he had been listening for—the sound of men entering the alley. Abruptly then, his gun drawn, the bodyguard Roy stepped through the doorway and moved to the left, his gun leveled. Maule followed him into the room with two bodyguards Pete had never seen before. Maule halted and looked searchingly at Pete, who said, "Hello, Ben. I just got back."

Maule didn't speak to him, shifted his glance to the sheriff and said, "Get out, Collie."

The sheriff rose now and left.

When he was gone, Maule looked at Pete and said, "You've got a lot to account for, my friend."

Pete nodded. "To you, but not to them," he said as he

tilted his head toward the three bodyguards. "Send them away."

Maule hesitated before saying over his shoulder, "Wait out in the alley. Shut the door."

When the two of them were alone, Maule moved over to the armchair and sat down. His broad face seemed a little shrunken and his green eyes were red-rimmed as if from loss of sleep or too much drinking. Momentarily, he was at a loss for words, as if he didn't know how to begin, and Pete offered no help.

"You've got a hell of a nerve coming back here," Maule said grimly. "And I aim to make you sorry for it." He paused. "You see, the stage driver saw Lace with you and you were helping her to escape."

"That's what Lefty and Beach told me," Pete said, nodding.

"Where are they?" Maule asked, puzzled.

"They were in jail until this morning until eleven o'clock. They'll be along."

"In jail? What for?"

"Why, I guess you'd call it for not believing me and Bill about picking up Lace. I hit Lefty for calling me a liar, then I had to take them both on. The sheriff locked them up for assaulting a law officer."

Anger and disbelief and confusion all showed in Maule's face and, beyond that, puzzlement was reflected there too. "What was your story of picking up Lace?"

Pete told the same story that Bill had told about their meeting with Lace and her account of losing her horse. He said almost with indifference, "She said since you'd booted her out she was heading west and could we give her a ride."

"Booted her out!" Maule exploded. "She escaped!"

"Now how were Bill and I to know that?" Pete asked. "Whenever she rides far from town you always send a couple of men with her, don't you?"

"Yes, and they weren't with her because she escaped."

"But they wouldn't be with her either if you'd kicked her out. Would they?"

Maule was fighting to control his anger and didn't speak immediately, his hard glare on Pete. "I don't reckon they would," he said reluctantly. "Still, didn't it seem funny to you that she wouldn't have hired a rig and a driver or taken the stage along with some trunks filled with her stuff?"

"She said she got out in a hurry because she was afraid you'd change your mind."

Maule pounced then. "So you were helping her escape. You were on her side."

"I was on your side," Pete said patiently. "You were done with her and had thrown her out. So you didn't want her pestering you. Helping her wasn't harming you, was it? I thought it was helping you."

"You drove straight through or else Lefty and Beach would have caught up with you."

Pete nodded. "Except for a change of horses at a relay. I planned to do that all along. I couldn't camp out with Shields, and if we slept at a relay station he might have got hold of a gun."

Maule said stubbornly, "Then why did you turn down my offer to send a couple of men with you? Was that because you knew you'd pick up Lace?"

"Back up a ways, Ben," Pete said coldly. "You knew Collier refused me the jail. You knew I had to get Shields to Indian Bend. She might have known I was going to Indian Bend, but how would I know she would be waiting out there in the road? I turned down your men because I was too proud to accept help, and you know it. He was my trouble, not yours."

Maule pondered this and Pete knew that while Maule couldn't refute anything Pete had said, he accepted all of it with the deepest reluctance.

Finally Maule said gloomily, "Then Lefty and Beach missed Lace?"

Pete nodded. "The San Francisco stage was making up

when we reached Indian Bend. I let her off at the stage office and then delivered Shields. When I got back the stage was gone."

"They didn't try to follow the stage?"

Pete shook his head. "I reckon they were more anxious to settle with me than find her. Of course they could have followed her after they got out, but by that time the stage would have a day's head start. I don't know what they did."

Maule said grimly then, "You couldn't have started that fight to delay them, could you?"

"I could have, but I didn't. If you told them you wanted Lace, why didn't they get a change of horses and follow her instead of laying for me?"

"I wanted you both brought back."

"Well, I'm back, but not with Lace, so what now?"

Maule didn't answer and rose and started a slow circle of the room, his hands clasped behind him, his head down as if counting the tile squares of the floor. When he closed his circle, he halted in front of Pete. "I'll wait until Lefty and Beach get back and hear their story."

"What if they lie to you?"

"Why would they?" Maule asked coldly.

"Because they couldn't handle either of the jobs you sent them to do. They got beat up and locked up like a couple of green cowhands."

"Sure you didn't put a gun on them there in the cell block?"

"They already had my gun. The sheriff made them leave theirs and mine on his desk before he let us in to hear Shields's story."

"We'll see what they say," Maule said.

Pete sighed. "Ben, we're going around in circles. The fact that I came back here means I'm telling the truth. There's nothing on my conscience. If there had been I'd have kept riding, wouldn't I?"

"Yes, there's that," Maule said reflectively. "Still, I can't see how you could swallow Lace's lies."

"And what do I know about Lace?" Pete asked, a touch of sarcasm in his question. "When I first hired on at th Crossfire, Josh Eddy said: 'If you got any notions about talking to Lace, forget them. If you got any notions of walking her home, forget it. Don't even talk to her except on business. She's Ben's girl.' I heard him real good."

"I still think you've left something out. There's something you haven't told me."

Pete allowed his temper to show as he said in disgust, "Ah, we've talked this to death, Ben." He rose now, facing Maule. "Here's what you do. Get Lefty and Beach's story. If it doesn't jibe with mine, send a man back to Indian Bend with some money. The county clerk there can write. Have your man pay him to take down Shields's version of what happened with Lace. Shields doesn't like you because you fired him and he doesn't like me because I shot him. So he just might say over again what he said to Lefty and Beach. If he doesn't, you can have my badge and my scalp."

For the first time since they had started talking, Maule smiled faintly. "You can bet I will." He turned now and went over to the door, paused and said, "Don't leave town, Pete. I'll be here watching you." He went out, closing the door behind him.

Pete sat down again. The worst was over and he didn't think Maule would move against him before he got the transcript of Shields's account of their meeting with Lace. Moreover, and best of all, Maule would be in town watching him when the first detachment of troopers arrived.

16

This was Laurie's morning to buy supplies for the kitchen. Usually Aunt Martha went with her, but last night Moynihan had come in drunk, fallen down stairs and had to be helped to bed by the two women. Sobering him up with coffee had robbed them of a precious hour of needed sleep which Aunt Martha wanted to make up before dinner preparations. So Laurie left the house alone with her list.

It was already hot and as she picked her way through the wagon traffic of Main Street, she held a handkerchief to her face against the always-present dust. Inside the oven of Otey Collins' store, she found the willing young clerk who always helped her and afterward delivered what she had ordered to the boarding house.

Buying food for the next one hundred and fifty meals that would be served before she bought again had first been an awesome job for Laurie to take on, but now she was adept at it. While the clerk rustled up the staples on her list, she discussed meat with the butcher. When the counter was piled high and the list was finished, she remembered they needed some material for making new dish towels. The goods counter was on the far side of the store and she headed through a cross aisle for it.

During the last few days, whenever she had been in the store, it had been her habit to look at the closed door bearing the sign MARSHAL'S OFFICE, and wonder what Pete was doing. After her talk with Moynihan, three days ago, she tried not to think of him, for he was gone, but habit persisted. She looked at the door, saw it was open and halted in her tracks. Were they cleaning it up after Pete's flight? Her

curiosity put her in motion and she walked down the aisle
and halted in the open doorway.

There, sitting in the chair facing the desk, was Pete Brisbin writing at his desk.

For a stunned moment Laurie could not believe what she
was seeing, but her joy won over her bewilderment as she
called, "Pete! Is it you?"

Pete swiveled in his chair, saw her, rose, and they met in
the middle of the room. Impulsively Laurie put out her
hand and they shook hands almost formally.

Then a torrent of words tumbled from Laurie's lips. "But
I thought you were gone for good with that woman. I
thought you'd be killed if you ever showed up here again. I
thought you were gone for good, for ever."

"Somebody's been talking way too much," Pete said
dryly. "Come over here and sit down, Laurie." Pete moved
past her, touching her shoulder with his hand with a kind of
extra greeting, moved to the door, closed it and then followed her until she had sat down in the armchair. Before
she turned and sat down, Laurie dabbed at her eyes with her
handkerchief. Whether it was relief at the sight of him or joy
that he had not fled with that gambling woman that brought
the tears, she didn't know or care. When she was seated,
Pete sat down and looked fondly at her. "Who's been talking about me, Laurie?"

"Moynihan said you'd run away with Lace Ferrill and
that Maule's men were after you and that Maule would kill
you if you ever showed up here again. Does Maule know
you're here?"

Pete nodded. "I talked with him last night."

"Can you tell me what happened?"

Pete told her just what he had told Maule the night before
and no more and, as he talked, Laurie wondered how she
could ever have believed Moynihan's harsh judgment of
him. He had done the kind thing, the right thing with Lace
and because he knew he had, he had returned to face
Maule's wrath. In fact, he had done everything Moynihan

said he wouldn't and couldn't do and hadn't done those things Moynihan had said he would do.

When he was finished, Laurie said after a moment's thought, "Then you're here on a kind of probation, is that it? Until Maule gets the report from Shields."

"That's it, Laurie. I can't leave town, but then I don't want to. And I'm still packing a gun."

"Shields can get you killed," Laurie said. "He's tried it once, so why wouldn't he let Maule try it again?"

"Maybe he will."

Laurie looked at him a long and puzzled moment before she said, "But you don't seem to care, Pete." She paused. "I'll never understand you, never."

"Tomorrow, you will."

"What does that mean?"

"I can't tell you, Laurie. But it will answer a lot of questions you've asked me before. Trust me."

"But you don't trust me," Laurie said.

"I do," Pete said soberly. "I don't want you involved, is all."

"But involved in what?"

Pete shook his head. "Forget it, Laurie. How's Aunt Martha?"

"You're treating me like a child," Laurie protested.

"Yes, like a very dear one. Now how's Aunt Martha?"

Laurie told him about Moynihan's drunk last night and was just finishing when a knock came on the door and the clerk opened it and poked his head around it. "I forgot how many yards, Miss Laurie."

"Four," Laurie said. Then she added, "No, I'll have to see how much four is."

She rose and said to Pete, "Then I'll see you tomorrow, Pete?"

"See me or hear about me, Laurie. But don't worry."

"I don't like that 'hear about me.' But I guess I can't do anything about it." She walked past him and unconsciously put her hand on his shoulder, as he had put his on hers, before she walked through the doorway.

Early that afternoon, Maule stopped by the marshal's office, entering the open door from the alley. This time, Pete noted, he had sense enough to tell Roy and the other two bodyguards to wait outside.

"Sit down, Ben."

"No, this won't take any time. Lefty and Beach got in a little while ago."

Pete watched his face, seeking a clue to his temper. It was grim, holding a controlled anger and frustration. "What's their story?"

"Not yours. They said Shields told them you and Lace planned her escape. You got mad because he gave you away and started beating him with his crutch through the cell bars. They jumped you and that's what started the fight."

"You believe them?"

"They brought the busted crutch," Maule said tonelessly.

"That I busted on Beach."

The two men looked at each other in unfriendly silence. Then Pete shrugged and said, almost with indifference, "I told you they'd lie."

"We'll find out. I sent a man out on the noon stage for Indian Bend. He'll bring back what Shields really said."

Pete nodded gravely. "That's fair of you, Ben."

"An hour after he gets back, I'll have lost one man—you, or two—Lefty and Beach."

"Don't be too rough on them, Ben. Remember, they're only trying to get even with *me,* not you."

His gall, or confidence, brought a look of fleeting admiration into Maule's eyes, and then they were neutral again.

"We'll see. Just stay around. Stay away from your horse too."

"I hear you."

Maule turned and went out.

17

As he had planned, Pete was getting a haircut in the small Mexican barbershop facing the main street early next morning. If necessary, he could stretch out the time with a hairwash and shave.

He was sitting in the barber chair, reading last week's tattered *Banner,* when he heard the sounds. It was unmistakable—the sound of many horses jogging almost in rhythm.

The barber ceased his work, saying, *"Oiga! Los caballerias!* The yellowlegs are come."

Pete turned his head and through the barbershop window saw the detachment of seasoned troopers, led by their officer followed by the guidon bearer, pass in a column of twos. Their horses were sleek, not yet sweating, and the troopers sat proudly in their saddles, knowing the attention they were attracting.

The two waiting customers moved to the door and they, the barber and Pete watched the detail pass and turn up the side street, heading for the sheriff's office on their first courtesy call.

When they had disappeared, Pete took off his apron, paid the barber, found his hat and stepped out into the street. His next move, he knew, was the critical one.

He headed for the Crossfire, cutting through wagon traffic and walking fast. On his way, he unpinned his badge and put it in his shirt pocket.

At the Crossfire, he asked of the first bartender, "Ben in yet?"

"Just come in."

The three bartenders watched with undisguised curiosity

as Pete hurried, almost ran, the length of the bar and entered the corridor. Although two of the four bodyguards were again Lefty and Beach, he did not even look at them or speak to them and they, trained by now, did not try to halt him or take his gun.

Maule's office door was open and he was seated at his desk going over yesterday's figures that Eddy gave him early each morning. Pete rapped smartly on the doorframe, startling Maule.

Without being asked in, Pete entered and closed the door. He didn't have to pretend to be breathing hard as he turned to Maule, for he was.

"Morning, Pete," Maule said. "What the hell are you so excited about?"

"Let me get my breath," Pete panted.

"Where's your badge?" Maule asked curiously.

Pete didn't answer. He reached in his pocket, showed it, then put it back.

Maule, knowing something was amiss with Pete, tossed the daily report on his desk and rose, frowning. "What's happened?"

Pete took a deep breath and came over to the desk. He took off his hat, wiped his forehead with his sleeve and put his hat back on. "Ben, do you think I've made a good hand for you?"

Maule stared at him, uncomprehending. "The best—until this last business, and maybe you're right on that. Why?"

"Then let me get out of town."

"Why?"

Pete took another deep breath and looked levelly at Maule. "You've wondered why I've kept my mouth shut about where I came from and what I was. Isn't that true?"

"Sure it's true, but I never blamed you."

"Well, you're going to find out more about me now, Ben." He paused to isolate this. "A detachment of cavalry troopers just rode into town. I can't let them see me."

A look of shocked disbelief came into Maule's face and

was washed out by a flickering fear that was instantly replaced by a look of caution. "You saw them yourself?"

Pete nodded. "They pulled up at the sheriff's office. But
they haven't seen me yet."

"Maybe they're just passing through. Find out."

"Damn it, Ben, I can't! Don't you understand?"

"Understand what?"

"One of my old outfit might recognize me!"

Maule looked at him searchingly but with a strange sym-
pathy, then cut around the desk, opened the door and
called, "Lefty." There were footfalls and then Maule said,
"Pete says the cavalry's in town. At the sheriff's office. Find
out why, and how long they're staying."

He closed the door and came around his desk and sat
down heavily. For some reason he stared at the report but
didn't pick it up. Then he raised his glance to Pete.

"When did you desert?"

"Two years ago. Fort Ely."

Maule only nodded. "Think we can hide you at Lace's
place?"

"It won't work, Ben. They'll learn there's a marshal here.
From Collier. Why hasn't he showed up? Why'd he disappear when we came? Then they'll be looking for me."

"See what Lefty finds out."

"If they stay, it's got to be Mexico for me, Ben. If you'll
let me go."

Maule only nodded; he really wasn't listening. He sat
there brooding, waiting, almost apprehensive, and Pete
knew he was thinking of his own plight.

Because he had to keep up some pretense of agitation,
Pete began to pace the floor. Presently, Maule asked, "You
get a good look at the troopers?"

"Good enough. Why?"

"They look like new recruits?"

"Anything but," Pete said bitterly. "A scattering of cor-
porals, some sergeants. No youngsters that I could see."

Maule frowned. "Doesn't sound like the ordinary detail."

"That's what worries me. They'd have to serve a couple or more enlistments to get those stripes. Then there's transfers." He added gloomily, "I could have served in the same outfit with any of them."

Maule only swore under his breath. It was getting to him, Pete knew. What he had just said could concern Maule as much as he pretended it concerned him.

When Lefty returned, he didn't bother to knock. He stepped into the room and closed the door behind him, and came directly to Maule's desk.

"They're from Fort Lyman and they're huntin' for deserters. They've had eight desertions in the last two weeks and they think that most of 'em headed for here. They'll bivouac north of town. Collie says they'll check the mines at every shift change, and the lieutenant was mighty happy they only had two saloons to watch." Now Lefty looked at Pete and said with dislike, "They want you to pay 'em a call, so you can help."

Pete and Maule exchanged glances as if they were two doomed men.

Maule said grimly, "That does it. Lefty, go get the horses. Bring Pete's too."

"You bringin' him?" Lefty asked.

"I said, bring his horse," Maule said roughly.

Silently, Pete again blessed that letter that the company clerk had written to Major Horton. Maule, indeed, was afraid to face the Army, especially those seasoned troopers Major Henderson had sent, one of whom might have identified him. Pete said now, in half hearted protest, "I can find my way down there alone, Ben."

"No, I'm going with you," Maule said, and then he smiled. "You see, you're not off my hook yet, Pete. I'll leave word with Josh to send Shields's statement down to us. I'll do it right now."

He rose and left the room and now Pete wondered how he could keep his word to Major Henderson that he would be riding beside Maule. Maule, of course, could place his men anywhere.

Maule was a long time with Josh Eddy, so long that Pete was worried Lefty and Beach would return with the horses before he could talk privately with Maule. However, the horses had not arrived when Maule returned to the room.

"How are you fixed for money, Pete?"

"I could use some."

Maule handed him a buckskin sack containing coins and said, "Let's call that an advance on your first month's salary."

Pete pocketed the coins and watched Maule seat himself, then said, "Ben, I've got a small favor to ask of you—small to you, but pretty big to me."

"Go ahead and ask it."

"When we ride out of here, can you put Lefty and Beach out in front of me?"

Maule looked at him carefully. "What you're saying is, you don't want your back to them."

"Yes."

"You think they'd do that in front of me?"

"I don't know. What I do know is that they are in big, big trouble when Shields's statement gets in your hands. They'll blame me."

There was a sound of several horses approaching in the alley and, when they were halted, Maule rose.

"You seem pretty sure of what Shields will say."

"I'm sure, and so are they."

Maule's lips were parted as if about to speak when the door opened and Lefty stuck his head in. "Everything's ready, Ben."

Maule looked at Pete, nodded imperceptibly, put his hat on and led the way out to the alley. Roy and three other men besides Beach were holding the horses. Pete wondered who the reinforcements were. When he noted the Circle M brand on the horses of the three strangers, he concluded they were Maule's cowhands Lefty had rounded up around town.

Maule stepped into the saddle and Pete, whose horse was already alongside his, mounted. As Lefty swung into his saddle, Maule said. "Lefty, you and Beach and Roy lead off."

That was the order in which they left the alley and the town itself—Lefty, Roy and Beach in the lead, Maule with Pete beside him, and the three Circle M punchers bringing up the rear.

Once they were clear of town, Pete settled into what he hoped passed for patience. But Maule, now that they were clear of town and the troopers, seemed relieved and talkative. He said that they would outfit Pete at the ranch and then head for the tiny Mexican town of Gertrudis across the border, where the natives were friendly, the girls pretty, the food awful and the bird shooting unbelievable.

Pete listened, thinking that if this came off, Maule had seen Gertrudis for the last time. He noted that they were beyond the spot where he had left the road the only time he had been out this way.

They topped a small rise that led abruptly down into an *arroyo,* when the front reined in as one. Two troopers and a cavalry officer, all mounted but halted, were in the middle of the road talking.

Maule said swiftly, "Ride on, you damn fools. There's only three of them."

Lefty, Beach and Roy pushed on ahead and the others followed.

"From the detachment in town?" Maule asked Pete.

"Have to be," Pete answered. Now they were close enough for Pete to recognize Lieutenant Blanton. He and his two troopers regarded them as they approached.

Lieutenant Blanton moved his horse forward toward them and reined in and, as they approached, held up an arm. This seemed to be both a signal for them to stop and a signal for the troopers to lift their carbines across their saddles.

Lefty turned his head. "He's stopping us."

"All right, be ready," Maule said.

The lead three came even with Lieutenant Blanton and reined in.

"You lost, Lieutenant?" Maule called pleasantly.

Blanton put his horse closer now and looked carefully at Maule, then at Pete.

"No, sir. My detachment is looking for deserters. If you'll look behind you you'll see more of my men. There are others ahead."

All of Maule's men turned and looked back. Four dismounted troopers, who had been hiding in the *arroyo* and had circled them, were standing on the crest of the road.

Maule turned his head around and looked at Blanton. "Looking for anybody in particular?" he asked pleasantly.

"Why, come to think of it, sir, yes—a sergeant deserter."

Now Maule turned his head and looked blandly at Pete. "Well, Pete, I tried to help you, but I don't like these odds. Better give yourself up to the lieutenant."

Blanton said mildly, "He's not a sergeant, sir, he's Lieutenant Peter Brisbin. The sergeant I'm looking for is named Jess Fairly, wanted for murder, grand larceny and desertion. He's going under the name of Ben Maule and I think they call you that in Banning, don't they?"

For a second, Maule sat utterly motionless, and then turned his head to Pete, a look of withering malevolence in his eyes. Then he called, "Let's go through 'em boys."

He roweled his horse savagely so as to put Lefty between him and the lieutenant, who was drawing his pistol from its holster.

"Fire when ready," Blanton called to his troopers.

The two troopers were raising their carbines when Lefty, his horse in motion, fired the first shot at them. The troopers fired back almost in unison and Lefty was driven out of his saddle.

Pete, crouching over in his saddle, hand on the holster of his gun, looked behind him at the three punchers. One of them was moving forward, almost half heartedly, the second had his hands lifted in surrender, the third was sitting motionless, surprise and confusion in his face. Pete knew that what they had heard of Blanton's words they had not understood, but they did know they were outnumbered by the troopers.

Pete put his horse in behind Maule's and now Beach, to his right, opened up on the troopers. Their close return fire hit Beach's horse and hit Roy. As Pete was passing Beach, he saw his horse rear and fall over backward.

Now Maule was alone and with a blind courage he headed straight for the troopers, shooting as he came closer.

One of his shots hit the trooper closest to him and the man dropped his carbine and tried to knee his horse out of Maule's way. The second trooper, who had surely been instructed by Blanton, raised his carbine, took sight on Maule's horse and fired. Maule's horse went down to its knees, pitching Maule over his head. And now Pete, his horse driving, swerved around Maule's horse. Maule had landed on his belly and, as he was driving to his feet, Pete swerved his horse in toward him, took his feet from the stirrups and then dove headlong on Maule.

The impact of Pete's body drove Maule down again on his belly. His arms were outstretched on the ground but he still held tight to his gun.

Pete, straddling Maule, put the whole weight of his body on his left arm, grinding Maule's face into the road. Now for the first time Pete reached for his gun and found his holster empty. He had lost it in the sprawling jump. He could feel Maule's body bucking under him trying to reach his knees and lift his head out of the choking dust.

Pete, knowing Maule would try to throw him off and shoot him, took a chance. He swung his right leg forward but could not reach Maule's gun hand with his foot. Throwing his body over Maule's head, he clawed his way down

Maule's arm, knowing what was inevitable. Maule's rump rose in the air as he got his knees under him and then, because he had to have some purchase with his hands, his right arm came back.

When it did, Pete reached out, grasped the barrel of Maule's gun hand and pulled it toward him, bending back Maule's hand to the point where the fingers had to spread and release the gun. It was then that Pete simply rolled off Maule and came to his feet, Maule's gun in his hand and pointing.

Lieutenant Blanton and the unwounded trooper, both afoot, came running up just as Maule rose.

Without a word and in the face of the leveled gun, Maule charged Pete. His drive was like a bull's, head down, legs driving, and Pete, sidestepping, brought the barrel of Maule's gun down across his kinky, dusty hair. Maule fell face down and lay motionless as Blanton and the trooper hauled up beside him.

"He's a rough one," Blanton said. "You all right?"

Pete was so winded he could only nod. Blanton put two fingers to his mouth and whistled shrilly and only now did Pete have a chance to survey the scene. The troopers had left their hill and walked down to take over the three Circle M hands. Beach lay under his dead horse and was making no effort to free himself. Roy was still mounted and his horse was walking in slow circles. Roy was hunched in the saddle with his arms wrapped across his belly, the reins still gripped in his left hand. Lefty lay on his back, arms and legs spread-eagled, while Maule's horse lay dead.

Now Maule groaned, rolled over and sat up, looking about him.

Lieutenant Blanton called to a newly arrived trooper, "Handcuffs, Corporal."

Maule, his face scratched and dirty, looked balefully at Pete. "I should have got you first."

"You should at that, Sergeant," Pete said.

* * *

Pete rode with the detachment as far as the business section of Banning and then he told Lieutenant Blanton that he would see him at the jail. Maule, handcuffed, his feet roped together under his horse's belly, had not spoken the whole way and he did not even look up as Pete left the detachment and headed up the side street leading past Mays's boarding house.

There would be no use describing the fight to Laurie, for it was nothing anyone would enjoy hearing. Lefty was dead. Beach had never made it free from his stirrups and his saddle horn had been driven into his chest when his horse went over, and he was dead. Roy, shot in the belly, was delirious and would not make it through the night. Lieutenant Blanton had instructions to post a heavy guard in the cell block of Sheriff Collier's jail. Tomorrow both detachments would ride back to Fort Lyman with their captive. Pete would have to be there.

When Pete walked into the boarding house, he went directly back down the corridor to the kitchen where the women were busy preparing dinner.

He stood in the doorway until Laurie saw him. With an exclamation of joy, she hurried to him. Aunt Martha heard her and looked around.

Laurie came into his open arms and Pete hugged her gently. Then, taking her by the elbow, he led her across the kitchen to Aunt Martha, who was frowning with disapproval.

"Aunt Martha, I would like to reintroduce myself. I'm First Lieutenant Peter Brisbin, Third United States Cavalry. My job here is done."

"And what was your job?" Aunt Martha asked.

"To capture Ben Maule and put him in jail. That was done this morning. He was a deserter, a killer and a thief."

"Well, I declare," Aunt Martha said softly.

Pete looked down at Laurie, who was watching him with a happy astonishment.

"I just wanted to get that out of the way, Aunt Martha, before I ask a question." He paused. "Do I have your permission to marry Laurie?"

He was watching Laurie as Aunt Martha said, "I didn't know you had asked her to marry you."

"I haven't, but I am. Now."

"In heaven's name, Lieutenant Brisbin, give her time to think about this."

To Laurie, Pete said, "I've been married before, Laurie. My wife died in childbirth. Does that make a difference to you?"

Laurie smiled and shook her head. "The first kiss is always supposed to be private, Pete, but this one won't be."

It wasn't.